"WHAT TURNS YOU ON?" ROBIN MURMURED, stunned to hear herself ask the question.

The warm glow in Patrick's eyes heated until it burst into flames. "You want to know what turns me on, Red? I'll tell you. Lying in your bed and wondering if you've ever made love under those silly glowing stars on the ceiling. Thinking about you on top of me, with your hair falling around us like a curtain."

Robin stared at him, transfixed. She knew she ought to turn and run, but she couldn't seem to tear herself away from his mesmerizing voice.

"And you know what else turns me on? Wondering if you have to lie down to zip those tight jeans you like to wear. Wanting to know if that sharp tongue of yours could be as inventive in bed as it is at spouting insults." His voice lowered to a sensual whisper. "But you know what turns me on most of all? It's knowing that I turn you on too. . . ."

WHAT ARE *LOVESWEPT* ROMANCES?

They are stories of true romance and touching emotion. We believe those two very important ingredients are constants in our highly sensual and very believable stories in the LOVESWEPT line. Our goal is to give you, the reader, stories of consistently high quality that may sometimes make you laugh, sometimes make you cry, but are always fresh and creative and contain many delightful surprises within their pages.

Most romance fans read an enormous number of books. Those they truly love, they keep. Others may be traded with friends and soon forgotten. We hope that each LOVESWEPT romance will be a treasure—a "keeper." We will always try to publish

LOVE STORIES YOU'LL NEVER FORGET
BY AUTHORS YOU'LL ALWAYS REMEMBER

The Editors

Loveswept® 647

WILD THING

BONNIE PEGA

BANTAM BOOKS

NEW YORK · TORONTO · LONDON · SYDNEY · AUCKLAND

WILD THING

A Bantam Book / October 1993

*LOVESWEPT® and the wave design are registered
trademarks of Bantam Books, a division of
Bantam Doubleday Dell Publishing Group, Inc.
Registered in U.S. Patent
and Trademark Office and elsewhere.*

*All rights reserved.
Copyright © 1993 by Bonnie Pega.
Cover art copyright © 1993 by Ed Tadiello.
No part of this book may be reproduced or transmitted
in any form or by any means, electronic or mechanical,
including photocopying, recording, or by any
information storage and retrieval system, without
permission in writing from the publisher.
For information address: Bantam Books.*

*If you would be interested in receiving protective vinyl covers for your
Loveswept books, please write to this address for information:*

*Loveswept
Bantam Books
P.O. Box 985
Hicksville, NY 11802*

ISBN 0-553-44257-0

Published simultaneously in the United States and Canada

Bantam Books are published by Bantam Books, a division of Bantam Doubleday Dell Publishing Group, Inc. Its trademark, consisting of the words
"Bantam Books" and the portrayal of a rooster, is Registered in U.S. Patent
and Trademark Office and in other countries. Marca Registrada. Bantam
Books, 1540 Broadway, New York, New York 10036.

PRINTED IN THE UNITED STATES OF AMERICA

OPM   0 9 8 7 6 5 4 3 2 1

Special thanks to licensed wildlife rehabilitators Lisa Sisk, Joanne D'Esposito, Sandy Mincz, and Pat Satterfield not only for answering my questions, but for the wonderful work you do.

ONE

"This isn't exactly the same as an injured raccoon," Robin McKenna said, looking over the man in the backseat of Joey's car and noting the white bandage on his temple.

"I know, Robin, but please let him stay," Joey Stockton requested. "He has a minor concussion, and Dr. Martin said someone needs to check on him every few hours."

"Why can't he stay with you?" She'd known Joey ever since she'd moved to Needle Ridge nearly five years ago and would stake her life on his honesty. However, something about the way he was refusing to meet her eyes aroused her suspicions.

"Marge has taken Betsy to visit her grandma over spring break, and I'm pulling double shifts at the veterinary clinic."

Robin had a bad feeling about this. "Who is he, anyway?"

"Trick Brady. I mean, Patrick Brady. He's Betsy's godfather. You've heard me mention him dozens of times. He came to spend a few days at the house to work on a st—on a project."

A voice suddenly rose from the backseat. "I'm glad the two of you are enjoying your chat, but I've got the very devil of a headache."

"Oh gosh, I'm sorry." Robin apologized. Imposition or not, he was still an injured man. "C'mon, we'll get you inside."

"I can manage." Patrick scrambled out of the car. He stood swaying for a moment, took one step, and his knees buckled.

Robin and Joey simultaneously grabbed his arms and steadied him. "Hell's bells!" Robin exclaimed. "Don't you have any sense at all?"

"I guess I need some help," Patrick muttered with the grudging manner of someone who wasn't used to asking for assistance.

"'Pride goeth before a fall,'" Robin said sweetly, then rolled her eyes at Joey. They stood on either side of Patrick and helped him inside the small cottage to the big brass bed that dominated one end of the oak-paneled room.

When he reached down to untie his shoes, Robin cleared her throat. "Ahem."

"What?" He barely glanced up.

"You haven't answered my question yet."

"What question?"

"About whether you have any sense or not."

"What?"

She jabbed a finger in the direction of his bandaged temple. "I just wondered, because it seems to me you could cause yourself a great deal of pain trying to do too much. But don't mind me. Go right ahead."

Patrick gritted his teeth against the pounding in his head. Much as he hated to admit it, she was right. And as much as he hated to ask for help, he did, even managing a smile and a thank-you. In a few minutes, Patrick was leaning back against several feather pillows, a glass of water and two tablets of aspirin in hand.

Robin frowned as she took in the sight of him. He looked at home, even amid the pink rosebuds on the sheets. His tousled dark hair was the kind that simply begged to have fingers threaded through it. Robin found her own fingers twitching in reaction. She glanced down at her hand and consciously folded it into a fist.

When she looked back up, she looked right into his eyes. Thick lashes fringed the most gorgeous golden brown eyes she'd ever seen. Eyes as sweet and rich as maple syrup. Eyes that were currently staring at her.

"Is that your real hair color?" he asked.

She blinked and glanced at Joey, who seemed to be watching the two of them with great interest, then said, "It is."

"Joey called you Robin. Is that because of your hair?"

"Because it's my name."

"I always had a soft spot for robins." Patrick closed his eyes. "Every spring our yard would be full of them. When I saw them, I always knew summer wouldn't be too far off. I love summer." He opened his eyes and looked at her, his gaze lingering on her hair. "I'd love to see your hair in the summer sun. I bet it glows like fire."

Flustered, Robin drew in a deep breath and cleared her throat. "Yes, well, um—" She turned to her friend. "So, Joey, what happened, anyway?"

Before Joey could say a word, Patrick interjected, "Why don't you ask me?" Patrick wasn't used to being ignored—especially by women. And he particularly didn't want to be ignored by this woman. He'd always had a penchant for redheads, and her hair was the most luscious shade he'd ever seen—copper-red shot through with streaks of pure gold.

"Okay. So what happened?"

"I had an argument with somebody."

"Some argument. Over what?"

"Over the distribution of the money in my wallet."

Robin cast another quick look at Joey, who had taken a seat in the rocking chair by the bed, a grin on his face, as if he was thoroughly enjoying this. "I see," she said carefully.

"Yessir." Patrick fastened his hands behind his head and crossed his jean-clad legs at the ankles. "He thought I should make some donations I didn't agree with."

"Charitable donations?"

"That's right. He thought I should make one to his wallet."

A corner of Robin's mouth twitched with a smile. "I suppose he won?"

Patrick shrugged. "He got the donation, if that's what you mean."

"But he had to hit you to do it."

"Ah, not exactly," Joey said.

Robin's eyebrows rose, and she glanced at Joey. "What do you mean by 'not exactly'?"

Joey's face split into a wider grin. "Trick got so mad at the guy that he took off after him, tripped over a manhole cover, and hit his head on the curb."

"A manhole cover? We only have two man-holes in the whole town."

"Well, one of them found me," Patrick grumbled.

"Jumped right out in front of you, did it?" Robin's eyes glittered with amusement.

That warm, contagious grin changed everything. Patrick nearly groaned aloud. Her sparkling hazel eyes and curving lips made him long to see what they'd look like when she'd been thoroughly kissed. By him. And there was that luscious hair of hers—hair that begged to be spread over a pillow. By him.

She was the sexiest woman he'd met in some time—maybe ever—but she wasn't for him. He traveled often and he traveled light—only one suitcase and no emotional baggage.

And yet somehow he knew it would be good with her. He wondered how she'd feel about a brief but hot fling before he headed back to civilization. Patrick mulled over this possibility as he watched Robin and Joey talk.

She had so much energy, she never stopped moving. Even sitting in a chair at the kitchen table with her legs crossed, she bounced one foot in time to some unheard melody. Her graceful hands gesticulated wildly as she talked. Even her hair moved. He fell asleep thinking of ways he'd like to rechannel that energy of hers.

The minute Patrick's eyes closed in sleep, she motioned Joey outside. "Look, if he's going to be around a day or two, then I want to know more about him. All I've ever heard you say about Trick Brady, besides that Betsy adores him, is that he's a city boy."

"He lives in D.C."

"D.C.? He *is* a long way from home, isn't he? What does he do?"

"He, ah, works in D.C. too." Joey glanced at his watch. "I've got to go. I have an afternoon surgery on one of Hooper's prize poodles. I'll call you later."

"Not so fast, Joey." Robin reached out and laid a hand on his arm. "I've known you ever since I moved here. Heck, you and Marge are my best friends. You've never lied to me yet, so don't start now. And don't evade my questions. What, exactly, does Patrick Brady do?"

Joey cleared his throat. "He's a, well, a reporter."

"*A reporter?*" Robin back away, horrified. "Oh, no, Joey. You know how I feel about reporters. I had to run as far as I could so they wouldn't completely destroy my life. And now you bring one here—*into my home!*" Her voice rose by degrees until the dog, who'd been dozing on the porch, came over and nudged her leg for a comforting pat.

She let a shaking hand rest on the animal's head. "Why didn't you tell me sooner?"

"Because I knew you'd react like this. Robin, all reporters aren't like the ones you ran into." Joey said earnestly. "Trick is honest and honorable. He's a good man and a brilliant investigative reporter."

Investigative reporter. Robin groaned. "I have news for you," she told Joey. "The words 'honorable' and 'reporter' are mutually incompatible. He can stay till tomorrow—then he's *out* of here."

"Fine," Joey sighed. "Look, wake him up every two hours to make sure he's okay. If he complains of nausea or severe pain, call Dr. Martin."

"You owe me one for this, Joey. You really owe me."

Robin slept in the rocking chair next to the bed. Every two hours she'd shake Patrick awake, and he'd look at her and murmur sleepily, "Hi, Red." Then he'd turn over and go back to sleep. She watched him for a while as he slept. Funny, he didn't look as if he could destroy her life. He did look as if he could change it, though.

Joey had been telling Robin for years how she'd really like Patrick. Mentally, she cataloged all the other things Joey had told her about his friend. She knew Patrick and his twin brother had gone through college with Joey, and she remembered Joey saying Patrick had graduated with honors. He'd described Patrick as motivated, idealistic, and honest to a fault. He traveled a lot, but kept in touch with his goddaughter nearly every week with cards, letters, and small gifts.

Finally, she dozed off again. She awoke at six o'clock, her usual wake-up time, took a quick shower, and changed into jeans, sweater, and leather boots. As soon as her steps sounded in the kitchen, the room seemed to come alive.

Tripod, a three-legged raccoon, uncurled from the pillow next to Patrick's head. Ritz, a one-winged mallard, stood from the nest he'd made in the puddle of material at the foot of the bed, Chanel, a descented skunk, watched with beady-eyed interest from the kitchen table. Robin smiled. The menagerie was out in full force this morning. She didn't usually let them stay in all night, but she'd been so preoccupied with Patrick, she'd forgotten to put the animals out in the shelter.

When she opened the pantry door, they all piled into the small kitchen and waited expectantly. Robin doled out their food, then tugged on sturdy gloves and hoisted a bag of kibble on one shoulder. Stuffing a handful of peanuts in one pocket, she grabbed a bag of chopped raw vegetables and went outside.

When Patrick awoke, he felt markedly better. The headache that had pounded all night, even through his sleep, was now an occasional throb when he moved.

He glanced at the clock—seven-thirty. Seven-thirty? He'd been known to go to bed about that time, but he'd never, at least not in recent memory, gotten up at that hour. Not a morning person by any stretch of the imagination, he usually slept till eleven, hit the streets about noon, returned home between seven and nine in the evening, and worked until three or four A.M.

There was very little worth getting up for at seven-thirty in the morning—except her. Patrick thought again of that tangle of red-gold flowing, no floating, down her back—the kind of hair a man could wrap around himself when he made love to her. And those eyes—one minute green, the next gold. Not his type of woman at all, he tried to tell himself. He preferred sophisticated women of the world who were looking for a pleasant evening, intelligent conversation, and good sex.

He sat up with great care and gingerly felt his bandaged temple, then held a hand out in front of his face. Five fingers. Good. Yesterday, he'd seen twice that many on the same hand. Feeling almost normal, he studied the room. It had rough-hewn wood walls and hardwood floors strewn with what his grandmother called "rag rugs." A rocking chair sat next to the bed, and a patchwork quilt hung over the brass footboard.

The refrigerator in the kitchen looked to be fifteen, maybe twenty, years old, and the stove even older than that. An old cast-iron pump perched over the sink, and in the middle of the kitchen table sat . . . a stuffed skunk!

Patrick closed his eyes for a moment, considering this unusual centerpiece. He opened them again and stared. It was definitely a black animal with a long, fuzzy tail and a white stripe. What a strange table decoration.

The kitchen door slammed, and the skunk jumped off the table. Patrick groaned. Perhaps the bump on his head was worse than they suspected.

Robin noticed Patrick right away. "You look better this morning," she said politely. "How do you feel?"

"Like the freight train running through my head has given way to a trolley."

When Robin grinned, Patrick stared at her, again captivated by the humor that curved her lips and danced in her eyes. He felt a stab of heat low in his body and began garnering his defenses.

"I'm glad. Maybe the trolley will give way to a motor scooter before long. Would you like some oatmeal?"

"With cinnamon? I'd love it."

"Good, I have some almost ready." She felt delighted he was so much improved. The sooner Patrick left, the better. When she set a tray in front of him, Patrick protested, "I can eat at the table."

"You might be dizzy, and I don't want you to take any chances."

"I'm going to eat at the table," he stubbornly insisted as he took the tray from her and walked over to the kitchen table with it.

Robin sighed. Patrick was as proud and independent as any creature she'd ever tended. It was just as well she'd had a lot of experience with wild animals. She knew to feed them when they got hungry, treat their injuries whether they wanted it or not. She knew never to take her eyes off them or trust them an inch, as they had an annoying habit of biting the hand that fed them. Most of all, she knew not to become too attached. All wild creatures eventually had to be set free.

Patrick Brady certainly had a healthy appetite. Robin watched as he scraped the last bit out of his second bowl of oatmeal. He'd already demolished three muffins and two glasses of orange juice. She found herself wondering if his other appetites were as healthy, then chastised herself for the very idea.

So the man was moderately attractive—she'd freely admit that. Okay, so he was more than moderately attractive. He was drop-dead gorgeous. Still, that was no reason to be fantasizing like a sex-starved spinster, she admonished herself as she cleared off the table. Carefully avoiding his eyes, she washed the few dishes, acutely conscious of his gaze on her.

"So what do you do out here in the boondocks?"

Robin had been so intent on ignoring Patrick that his voice startled her, and she nearly dropped the juice pitcher. "I'm a licensed wildlife rehabilitator."

As Patrick stretched out his legs, the denim pulled tightly over his powerful thighs. "What does a licensed wildlife rehabilitator do?"

"Rehabilitate licensed wildlife," she said wryly. "What did you think?"

"So that *was* a skunk in the middle of the table." Patrick sounded satisfied—and relieved.

"That was Chanel."

Patrick chuckled. "Chanel, hmm? Appropriate. How do you keep her from, well, you know."

"She's been descented. That's why I can't release her back into the wild—she'd be defenseless."

"How many other not-quite-rehabilitated creatures do you have around here?"

"Just a few. Most of the animals I get, I eventually can return to their native habitat."

"And if you can't?"

"If I can't, then I usually find a home for them at a wildlife preserve or nature park. Otherwise there can be problems—especially with deer."

"Why?"

"They become so tame that they lose all their fear of man—and wind up as venison on a hunter's table."

She didn't look much like a wildlife rehabilitator, Patrick mused. More like a model. The tight, faded jeans she wore outlined delicious curves and heartbreakingly long legs, and her bulky oversize sweater only highlighted the slender, supple body beneath. She wasn't classically beautiful—her features were too animated and alive for the ice-maiden look. She was, instead, warm and captivating.

Patrick crossed one leg over the other and steepled his hands as he watched Robin tidy the small kitchen area. A bundle of restless energy, she went from one activity to another without stopping. Laid-back and casual himself, Patrick was intrigued by Robin's quick, agile movements.

"Do you mind?" she stood in front of him, mop in hand.

"Go right ahead," he replied easily, though he didn't move from the chair. "I don't mind at all."

"Well, I do. You're in my way. Why don't you go for a walk or something until Joey comes to pick you up?"

Patrick got out of the chair, but went over to sit on the edge of the bed instead. Yesterday, he hadn't been thrilled at spending even a night or two in the back of beyond. Now the idea of leaving appealed even less. He wanted to learn more about the fascinating Miss Robin McKenna.

He wondered if she knew how much her eyes gave away. If the eyes were really mirrors to the soul, then her soul lay bare for all to see. Her eyes were, by turns, warm and cool, merry and solemn, open and wary. Currently they regarded him with a fair measure of distrust. He wanted to assure her he was as honest as a Boy Scout, but it would be a lie.

He took great pride in the stories he'd written exposing political corruption. And if he'd had to resort to a little subterfuge occasionally, then so be it. He didn't pretend to be lily-white. He simply hated secrets—and had an amazing talent for uncovering them.

Patrick stretched and got to his feet, wincing a little at the residual stiffness from his fall. Maybe Robin would let him have a hot shower before he left. The way she viciously attacked a stray smudge on her floor, however, he wasn't sure she'd agree. She seemed prickly—as if she couldn't wait for him to leave.

"Do you mind if I take a shower?" he asked politely.

She barely glanced up. "Go ahead. Towel's on the shelf over the sink." When he headed toward the bathroom, she looked up long enough to say, "The door doesn't close all the way. There's a warp in the floorboard."

"Are you planning to spy on me while I wash?" Patrick gave a wicked smile as color suffused her cheeks. He found her blush an enchanting novelty.

With the door ajar Robin could hear every sound Patrick made—the rasp of his zipper being lowered, the whisper of the denim as he removed his jeans. When her thoughts strayed to what those jeans had been covering, she took a deep breath. "Well," she muttered to the raccoon, who waddled over to investigate the streaks of water on the floor, "it's certainly time for me to finish the rest of my chores. Past time." Tugging on her leather gloves, she returned to the outdoors.

Fifteen minutes later she came back inside to get antibiotics and a change of dressing for the injured fox she was nursing. As she opened the door, Ritz darted in, flapping his one wing in excitement. He headed straight for the bathroom door.

"Uh-oh." Robin made a grab for him, but the duck ran under the kitchen table and out the other side. "Patrick—" she called out to warn him, but he couldn't hear her over the water. Then she heard a muffled "What the hell?" and a loud thump.

She cringed and ran the few steps to the bathroom door. "Patrick? Are you all right?"

"Just dandy," he said sarcastically.

Robin peered around into the bathroom. All six-feet-plus of gorgeous naked male lay on her bathroom floor, clutching a towel. "Oh my goodness!" Part of her absently wondered how he'd got so tanned all over. Her mouth went dry. There seemed to be so *much* of him.

"Oh gosh, I'm sorry," she said lamely. "I should have warned you about the duck. He loves showers."

Glancing pointedly at the duck standing under the spray of water, Patrick sat up and draped the towel discreetly over his lap. "What do you do for encores, lady? Skunks on your tables, ducks in your showers. Do you have bees in your bonnet, as well?"

"You don't have to get testy," she replied defensively. "It's not like I sicced him on you on purpose. Now, what's wrong?"

"When that creature jumped in the shower with me, I jumped out and slipped on something. I think I broke my ankle."

Robin glanced at the ankle and winced. It *did* look swollen. "I think I'd better call Dr. Martin."

"Would you help me into the other room first? I'm not exactly comfortable lying on the floor."

Robin immediately bent down to help him up, then stopped short at the sight of all that male flesh. Water droplets still sparkled on his shoulders and in the crisp brown curls on his chest. He had great legs—long and lean and muscled and dusted with brown hair. She drew in her breath.

"Oh hell, I'll do it myself," Patrick said when she hesitated. Keeping one hand on the towel, he used the other to grab the edge of the sink and lever himself up. He stood balancing on one foot as he secured the towel around his waist. "You're acting like you've never seen a naked man before."

Robin let out the breath she'd been holding. "I, um, well, not recently, no."

Patrick felt a curious satisfaction—that meant she wasn't involved with anyone at present. "Do you like what you see?"

"Oh yes . . ." She stopped in obvious embarrassment. "I mean, it's fascinating. I didn't know one man could wear that much arrogance. If little else," she finished tartly.

"Truce, truce." Patrick held up his hands. "It's getting a little difficult to balance on one foot. Could you please help me?"

Her face softened. "Are you in much pain?"

"My ankle's pretty numb right now."

"I guess that's good." Robin bit her lip. "How should we do this?"

"Why don't you stand on my good side, and I'll lean on you?"

"Sure. Let me cut off the shower first." She

reached over and turned off the water, ignoring the duck, who let out a disgruntled quack. "Okay." She moved to Patrick's side, and he draped an arm around her shoulders.

"Now hook your arm around my waist," Patrick urged.

Robin complied, her fingers immediately pressing into the warm, damp skin at his side. Her heart pounded, and her breath came in short pants, but she told herself it was only because she was closer than she ever cared to be to a reporter.

They managed to get across the few feet of floor between the bathroom and the bed. When Patrick turned around to sit on the edge of the mattress, somehow Robin's feet got in the way, and they ended up falling on it instead.

"Ohmigosh! Patrick, are you all right?"

"My ankle hurts too much for me to be dead, so I guess I'm okay." He opened his eyes to find hers about four inches away. "And getting better every minute."

Despite the twinges of pain he was obviously feeling, Robin could see desire tighten his features and suddenly realized the position they were in: Their bodies wedged tightly together, her breasts nestled against his arm. One of his bare legs snuggled between her jean-clad thighs, and she felt the warmth of his breath against her face.

Their eyes met and held. Robin couldn't look away, couldn't move away. Their bodies fit together as if they were two matching pieces of a puzzle. His gaze shifted from her eyes to her lips, and his head bent toward hers. His lips brushed over hers once, twice, the lightest of kisses.

She wanted more. She *needed* more. But that very need made her gasp, untangle herself, and scramble to her feet. Her chest heaved with something besides exertion as she said, "I'm glad you're all right. Can I, um, do something to make you more comfortable?"

Patrick's eyes swept over her in an appreciative look. "Not now, Red. I have a headache," he murmured with a wicked grin. "But soon. Real soon."

Robin glued on a professional manner to mask her inner turmoil as she helped Patrick get settled in the bed. Then she placed a call to Dr. Martin. When she turned back to Patrick, she said coolly, "He said he'd run by at lunch to look at your ankle. In the meantime, you're to keep off it, keep it elevated, and keep ice on it."

Fleeing Patrick's amused eyes, Robin stepped out on the porch to think. Several things bothered her. One was Patrick's self-satisfied smile. Another was that it didn't look as if he would be going anywhere for at least a few more days. She couldn't say she was thrilled, but she would have expected to be more upset about it. That she wasn't, bothered her most of all.

TWO

Robin stood on the porch and watched the doctor drive away. She should be glad it was only a sprain. Had the ankle been broken, Patrick would be around longer than just a few days. He'd offered to go to Joey's, but with Joey at the clinic and Marge gone, there'd be no one to take care of Patrick. So Robin insisted he stay with her. After all, it had been her duck.

She fixed him lunch, again marveling at his appetite. He wolfed down two grilled ham-and-cheese sandwiches, two mugs of tomato soup, and an apple. Robin was tempted to lift up the corner of the sheet to see where he was putting all that food. Only with his clothes currently in the dryer, she knew exactly what was under the sheet.

"Terrific lunch." Patrick handed her his tray and stretched. Robin watched the play of muscle across his bare chest, her gaze lingering on the smattering of soft brown curls. She had a crazy desire to reach out a finger and see if they were as silky as they looked. She knew she was staring and forced her eyes up, only to meet his smile.

If his chest was gorgeous, his smile was devastating. And when he saw her wide-eyed scrutiny, that smile broadened. Robin made herself take the tray into the kitchen. *What is the matter with me?* she thought.

She'd seen him virtually nude in the bathroom earlier, and that had been disconcerting enough. But her attention had soon been diverted to his injury. Now, however, his wickedly male smile, and the memory of the physique that lay beneath the sheets posed a pure irresistible danger. She only hoped that he hadn't noticed her fascination.

Patrick had noticed, all right. The air jangled with feminine awareness. He'd been conscious of her innate sensuality from the first moment he'd seen her—a sensuality that seemed as natural to her as breathing. Now every nerve in his body had tuned in to her frequency.

Bad timing. He had an overdue story to finish and an anxious editor to deal with. He didn't need to be thinking about chameleon eyes, small, firm breasts, and the longest, sexiest legs he'd ever seen.

Robin turned around again and caught him staring. "Did you want anything else?"

Lots, Patrick thought, but he wasn't in any shape to do anything about it. Not yet. "Well, I could use a shave." He scratched at his chin. "I didn't get to it this morning before the duck. And I'd love to brush my teeth."

Robin hurried out of the room to search for an extra toothbrush. Maybe with a toothbrush hanging out of his mouth and lather dripping down his chin, his smile would be less effective. She could only hope. Just what was there about his smile that made it so appealing? A certain boyish charm, she decided, combined in the most confusing way with sheer male arrogance.

She set a toothbrush with a dab of toothpaste on it, a cup of water, and a basin in front of Patrick. "What do you need to shave with?"

"Would a mirror, a soapy washcloth, and a razor be too much trouble?"

Mister, watching you make yourself at home in my bed is too much trouble. "Just a sec."

When Robin came back with the items, he'd already finished brushing his teeth. There was a dab of toothpaste lather at the corner of his mouth. Robin stared at that dab for a long, frozen moment, imagining running her tongue around his mouth, savoring the minty taste.

No, no, no! She clamped down on her runaway imagination. She'd never in her life had this kind of reaction to a man. Her response to her husband had been maybe a tenth as powerful, and look what had happened—her good sense had gone sailing right down the bay.

Obviously she didn't have the necessary skills to deal with men. In college, Greg Royal had only kissed her a few times, and she'd nearly given him the answers to Professor Barron's biology exam. It had been even worse with her husband. John Douglas's lame excuses had been cushioned by the sweetest talk, and she had become deaf, blind, and infinitely stupid.

Never again. She'd worked too long and too hard to have her plans jeopardized by a little chemistry. There was too much at stake to let a man—especially a reporter—get in the way.

Robin handed the razor to Patrick, who held it up for inspection. "Tell me, Red Robin, you haven't used this on your gorgeous legs, have you?"

"Of course not!" Robin glared at him and pointedly turned her back, going over to the clothes dryer.

"Hey, wait!" Patrick called after her.

He could see the reluctance in her face as she turned back. "Yes?"

"I'd love to sit out on your porch this afternoon. If it's not too much trouble."

Robin nodded curtly. "I have a few things to do now, but it shouldn't take but a couple of minutes. That'll give you time to finish shaving." She wished he wouldn't be so mannerly. Her life would be much simpler if she could hate him. Removing the clothes from the dryer, she stuffed them in the laundry basket, and left the room.

When she returned a few minutes later, she noticed several tiny nicks on Patrick's face. "Did you get the name of the cat that ran over your face?"

"Very funny." Patrick stared at his face in the mirror. "I just haven't used an old-fashioned razor in years."

"Are you ready to get up now?"

"I'd love to, but it might be better if I had some pants on. I don't want to catch cold from the draft."

"Heaven forbid," Robin murmured dryly. She turned and began searching through the laundry basket for his briefs. Her cheeks grew warm when she found them nestled up to a pair of her lacy panties. She tossed his underwear at him and immediately turned her head. "I trust you can manage these by yourself."

"Would you help me if I couldn't?" Patrick asked with amused interest.

"If you couldn't dress yourself, you could walk around wearing the sheet off the bed, for all I care."

"Or wearing nothing at all."

Robin pointedly ignored his rejoinder. "Your jeans are hanging over the foot of the bed." The whisper and rustle of the denim being tugged over his legs was the sexiest thing she'd ever heard—next to the sounds he'd made removing the jeans. "Your shoes are—you probably won't be able to get on your shoe, will you?"

"I'll just wear my socks. After all, I'm not going far."

True, she thought. She wondered if "out of sight, out of mind" still held when someone was indelibly etched on your memory.

"Do I have a clean shirt?"

"You should. Joey brought your suitcase yesterday."

"Oh. Could you grab a shirt for me?" Patrick winked at her. "Preferably one that matches my eyes."

"Bloodshot brown? I don't think so."

"You're a pill." His grin belied his words.

The warm grin went straight to Robin's head,

making her feel giddy. "I have to be. You're a headache."

"So we go well together."

That's what I'm afraid of, Robin thought. This verbal fencing, however entertaining, had to stop. As a matter of fact, it had to stop *because* it was entertaining. She put on her most professional manner and dug a shirt out of the suitcase. "Here."

"Thanks."

Robin watched surreptitiously as Patrick stuffed his arms in the sleeves and buttoned the shirt about halfway. Shoot, the man could even make putting *on* clothes seem sexy.

"Okay, lead on." He offered his arm with all the finesse of a prince.

"I'm not the walking wounded here." Robin offered her arm instead.

Patrick slid his arm slowly between her arm and her body, managing to brush the side of her breast as he did so. Robin gave him a sharp look, but he only smiled, an innocent butter-wouldn't-melt-in-his-mouth smile. She held her arm a little farther from her side.

When Patrick sat in the rocking chair on the porch, she offered to go back in and get a footstool to prop up his ankle. "I'm fine like I am," Patrick insisted.

"I know. You're ready for the Boston Marathon and all that. I'll get the footstool anyway."

"Fine," he grumbled. "If it'll make you happy."

"It'll make me ecstatic."

Patrick cast a sideways glance at Robin. "I'd love to see you in the throes of ecstasy." He saw the flustered look on her face as she went back inside and decided he liked disconcerting her a great deal.

He still wasn't sure why he was so taken with her. Usually he liked women to be curvy and amenable and elegant. Robin was slender and acerbic and casual. Yet he felt stimulated both mentally and physically in a way he hadn't been in years.

She moved with an easy grace that seemed as natural to her as breathing. And her casualness suited her. He doubted very much that she would ever complain about a man's kisses smearing her makeup or mussing her hair.

A man would certainly have to keep on his toes to match her sardonic wit. A relationship with her would be exciting, irritating, exasperating, exhilarating. It might have the ups and downs of a roller-coaster ride, but it would never be boring. He just now realized how boring all those compliant former debutantes were.

Robin tucked a footstool with a pillow under his ankle. "So what do you think of my mountain?"

A light, cool breeze fluttered the long needles on the graceful pines that gave Needle Ridge its name. The wildflowers in the meadow in the distance were a palette of primary colors—yellow buttercups, wild blue lupines, red and yellow columbines. Patrick breathed in air so clean and sharp, it almost hurt, then tilted up his head to feel the warmth of the sun on his face. "It's beautiful. I'm not used to such wide open spaces, though."

"Have you always lived in the city?"

"I grew up in the Maryland suburbs outside D.C. There were beautiful houses and well-landscaped lots but—"

Her face darkened for a moment. "I know what you mean."

Patrick glanced at her. "I can't imagine you living in suburbia."

Robin smiled, but Patrick noted little mirth. "Well, I did. I know all too well the impeccably manicured lawns, the carefully arranged flower beds with the obligatory geraniums set by the decks with the obligatory wicker furniture."

"I take it you didn't like it much better than I did," Patrick remarked.

"I hated it!"

There was so much vehemence in her tone that Patrick stared. She'd probably refuse to answer, but he had to ask. "Why?"

She looked at him a long moment, her eyes carefully assessing, then said slowly, "Because it forces people into little molds. Only it sometimes turns out that the real people were camouflaged by their uniform lifestyles, and they're nothing like you thought."

What had happened to put so much disillusionment into her voice? he wondered. "Robin, what—"

"I have millions of chores to finish," she interrupted him. "Think you'll be happy here for a couple of hours?"

"I could look at this view all day." But Patrick knew he wasn't at all interested in the view. Every time he found out something new about Robin, it brought up more questions. She wasn't exactly forthcoming about herself. He sighed. Of course, neither was he. He shifted in the chair and tried to take in the view.

Fifteen minutes later, he yawned and glanced at his watch. Enough scenery for one day. He had a low boredom threshold, and this was pushing it to the limit. It was time for a little entertainment.

He'd already noticed a severe dearth of entertainment materials. No television, no CD player, not even a radio. How anyone could survive without them, he didn't know. In D.C., he usually had his television tuned in to either the twenty-four-hour news network, the sports channel, or MTV. And on the rare occasions he wasn't relaxing with television, it was because he had on the VCR instead.

"Robin?" he called out. "Robin!"

"What's wrong?" She appeared a few seconds later from the side of the house. She tucked her gloves in her back pocket as she hurried over to Patrick. "Are you all right?"

"Do you have something I can read?"

"That's it? The way you bellowed, I thought something was horribly wrong. After all, you said you could look at this view all afternoon."

"So I overestimated the time a little."

Robin just shook her head, went inside, and came back out with a rolled-up newspaper. She tossed it in Patrick's lap and headed back around the corner of the house.

"Hey, wait!"

"What now?" She sighed and turned around again.

"This paper's six days old."

"So? That's the latest issue. Up here we don't get a daily." Robin smiled sardonically at the look of utter horror that flitted across Patrick's face. "Must be quite a shock to find out there are people who don't even care about daily papers. Especially for a reporter like you, fighting for truth, justice, and the American way. Makes you sound a bit like Superman, don't you think?" She turned and walked around the side of the cottage.

Patrick stared after her. Well, that was clear as a bell. Robin McKenna obviously didn't like reporters. But why not?

Robin remained distant all during dinner, though she managed to be pleasant. Afterward, she cleared off the kitchen table and spread out some paperwork. Patrick retreated to bed with a copy of *Small Mammal Care*. It told him everything he'd never wanted to know about taking care of small animals. After an hour or two of reading about the essentials of raising young rodents, he looked over at Robin. "Can I help you do something?"

Robin looked up from her stack of papers. "Hmm? Oh, no, thanks. It's a revised grant proposal."

"Grant proposal?"

She laid down a much-chewed pencil. "Every year the Webster Foundation in Richmond allocates a certain amount of money for projects dealing with wildlife preservation. I could really use the money. They're interested in my proposal, but need more detailed figures. They want to make a decision in the next week or two."

"I hadn't thought about it before, but I guess you don't get paid much, do you?"

"Much?" Robin snorted. "Wildlife rehabilitators don't get paid at all."

"Not a cent?"

"Not a cent. We get by almost completely on private donations."

"But the food . . . vet bills . . ."

"Unless I get donations, it all comes out of my own pocket."

"Is it like this everywhere?"

"As far as I know." Robin picked up the pencil again and absently chewed on the end. "I don't know of anybody who gets paid for it."

Respect dawned in Patrick's eyes. She put in a lot of hard work and long hours for a pittance. "So you do it because you love it."

Robin smiled. "I'd better love it. It's not always fun, but it's something I feel is right. Maybe, in some small way, I can help make amends for what we're consciously or unconsciously doing to this world of ours."

"I guess we do treat the planet as if we could

go buy another at the corner drugstore, don't we?
A lady I did a story on last year said that. She lives
over on the Eastern Shore and travels all over the
U.S. to help in cleaning up waterfowl caught in oil
spills."

"Ila Hatcher."

"Yeah. Do you know her?"

"Not really, but I've heard of her. I heard her
speak once in Norf—Tidewater. She's quite a
lady."

"So are you, Robin." She ducked her head so
he couldn't see her face. "You know, Ila said that
my article brought in several thousand dollars in
donations. Maybe I could do an article about
you—"

Her head jerked up. "*No!* I mean, thanks but
I'm a very private person, and, um, I'm sure that
with the grant and all I'll be able to manage fine."
Part of her had to admit that it was a kind offer on
his part. He just didn't know the can of worms
he'd be opening if he did that.

Patrick shrugged. "If you change your mind,
let me know. How do most wildlife rehabilitators
manage without money?"

"Most rehabilitators are married women who
are staying at home with kids anyway. And local
vets are usually willing to donate their services—
like Joey does for me. Occasionally people who

bring over an animal contribute money toward its care."

"How do you manage? You're not married."

"I have some income from my father's estate that allows me to do this—provided I'm fairly frugal. And I get a little help from the people in town on occasion." She took a deep breath. "But that grant would sure come in handy."

"What would you do with it?"

Her eyes lit up. "I'd like to open an actual wildlife center. Not just to take care of injured animals—I'd be able to educate the public too. Maybe I could work with some of the national wildlife organizations to educate people about protecting endangered species. I have a special interest in that."

Patrick stared at her a long moment. Robin looked as wistful as a little girl adoring a beautiful doll in a department-store window. He wanted to promise her that she'd get her grant, that she'd win the lottery—anything, so she could achieve her dream.

Robin shifted uncomfortably under Patrick's intense scrutiny. Finally, she smiled a little and turned back to her papers, stacking them neatly. "Well, enough about what I want to be when I grow up. How about you?"

"Me? I don't know," Patrick murmured

thoughtfully. "I've always wanted to do a series of illustrated magazine articles—and provide not only the copy but the pictures as well."

"Are you also a photographer?"

He shrugged disparagingly. "I play around with it some."

"What do you like to take pictures of?"

"Kids and animals, believe it or not. They're both completely natural and without artifice. When you take their picture, you see exactly who they are."

That answer totally disarmed Robin, but she couldn't resist saying, "I'd have thought you wouldn't like kids or animals."

"I don't." She saw what might have been a twinkle in his eye.

"Well, um, morning comes early, you know. Good night, Patrick." She stood and nodded in his direction.

"Good night, Red Robin." He loved the way she said his name. She made it sound like a caress, even when she didn't intend to. With a sigh he turned back to the care and feeding of baby rabbits.

"Aargh!"

Robin awakened from a dead sleep. What was

wrong? She sat up in bed and listened. She heard a thump, then a muffled curse.

Shoving her feet into fuzzy slippers, Robin padded down the rough oak stairs. She found her way easily in the dark. "Hell's bells! What's all the racket?"

Patrick sat straight up in the bed, the bare skin of his torso looking dark and shadowy in the moonlight that gleamed through the window. "There was something sitting on my chest."

Robin turned on the lamp next to the bed. Patrick blinked, then fastened his eyes on Robin. She wore a voluminous red flannel gown that contrasted vividly with her hair. He sighed. The heavy gown covered everything it was supposed to all too well, only barely hinting at the curves of hip and breast.

Robin indicated the large orange tabby who sat, tail twitching, at the foot of the bed, apparently irritated by all the hoopla. "I think it was Rosie."

Patrick snorted and lay back down, turning over on his side. He started upon seeing a small white cat who was curled up on the other pillow, her serene amber eyes staring back. "Good God!" The white cat started to purr and began washing her paws.

"That's Pooh. As in 'Winnie the.'"

"Sure," Patrick murmured. A small noise from the floor next to the bed drew his attention. When he leaned over, he saw a raccoon curled up on top of his discarded socks. Leaning back on the pillow, Patrick gazed up at the ceiling, almost expecting to see more furred faces peering out from around the wooden support beams. "I take it back. You don't have bees in your bonnet. You have bats in your belfry. Can I ask you a silly question?"

"Go right ahead."

"Why are there stars on your ceiling?"

Robin glanced up at the glowing star-shaped decals. "I like feeling like I'm outdoors when I sleep."

"That's right," Patrick said in satisfaction. "This *is* your bed."

"Of course it is. You haven't exactly been in condition to climb up to the guest loft," Robin retorted.

Patrick's eyes narrowed as they again swept down the flannel nightgown to the tips of the fuzzy slippers peering out from beneath the hem. "I like sleeping in your bed," he murmured. "I wonder what it would be like to make love in this bed. Hmm?"

Robin spun around and grabbed Rosie in one

hand, Pooh in the other. "It's late. Good night."
She marched back upstairs.

"Hey," Patrick called after her. "You forgot
to turn out the light."

"So sue me!"

Patrick grinned. He enjoyed sparring with
her. She was spectacular when she was flustered
or miffed. Her cheeks flushed an enchanting
rose; her well-shaped breasts heaved. Her hair
fairly crackled around her, and her eyes turned
from hazel to gold. Patrick decided he was partial
to gold eyes.

He reached out and pulled the chain on the
old-fashioned brass lamp, then lay back, looking
up at the glowing decals on the ceiling. Her bed.

He turned his face into the pillow, inhaling
the sweet fragrance—the same one he'd noticed
when she'd fallen with him on the bed. It was her
hair, he thought, and closed his eyes. Patrick
could imagine weaving his fingers through the
froth of red-gold curls, bringing handfuls of her
hair to his face so he could breathe in that sweet,
delicate scent.

He thought of lying with her on this bed, their
bare legs entwined together and his fingers en-
meshed in that tangled curtain of hair. He'd
spread those tresses over her creamy breasts, so
her delightful pink nipples would barely peek

through. They'd have to be pink, he mused fancifully. That was the only color that would go with her hair and that pale honey-cream skin.

A sudden swelling tightness in his lower body caused him to open his eyes and stare at those silly stars on the ceiling. He couldn't sleep, and it was all her fault. Her and her absurd hair, almost too much for her slender body. Almost. But not quite. It was just the right amount of hair to wind his hands through to anchor her face for his kiss.

He shifted uncomfortably as he felt another stab of desire. Sighing, he stared at the orange numerals on the clock. No wonder he wasn't sleepy. Two A.M. didn't often find him in bed—at least not to sleep. He reached over and turned the light back on.

With no television, he figured he'd have to read. He got out of bed and gingerly hobbled around. He hoped he'd find a magazine, or some books—on something other than animal care—or he'd go stir-crazy before morning.

He picked up a book on the kitchen counter. *Animal Husbandry in the Nineties.* He set it back down. What in the world did Robin do with her time? With nothing besides her grant proposal and those gosh-awful books for company, why hadn't she gone stark raving bonkers by now?

His ankle twinged in protest, so he limped

back over to the bed and sat down. He glanced at a book lying on the nightstand and shook his head. He was not reading *Caring for Small Rodents*. In boredom, he tugged open the nightstand drawer. Maybe she kept a book in there.

The drawer was a jumble of pens, pencils, old letters, and makeup containers, but no books. Disgusted, he shut the drawer again, but dislodged a piece of paper as he did. It was a yellowed newspaper clipping. He glanced at it casually, preparing to stuff it back in the drawer, when he noticed the accompanying picture.

It was Robin. He read the caption. "Teresa Exbury leaves the chapel after attending services for her husband, John Douglas Exbury, who died Monday."

Patrick stared at the picture, his reporter's eye noticing details anyone else might have overlooked. He'd wager that black designer suit she was wearing had cost the equivalent of his weekly salary. And the silver BMW waiting at the curb wasn't exactly cheap either.

His brow creased in thought, he tucked the paper back in the drawer and turned out the light. Teresa Exbury. So pretty little Robin McKenna wasn't really Robin McKenna. Instead, she was the pretty little Widow Exbury. Why the charade?

And if she could afford designer suits and silver BMW's, why was she living in surroundings one step above poverty level? Why did she need the grant money so much?

John Douglas Exbury. There was something about that name, something Patrick couldn't quite put a finger on. It had been in the news—he was sure of that. And had Robin been in the news too? By five A.M., when sleep finally claimed Patrick, he hadn't come up with the answer.

Even though her sleep had been interrupted, Robin still bounced out of bed at her usual time. She was a morning person in every sense of the word. She preferred the early melody of the mockingbird to the evening ballad of the whip-poorwill, the increasing warmth of dawn to the growing coolness of nightfall. She found sunrises vastly superior to sunsets and liked knowing that a whole day of sunshine lay ahead, rather than a long evening of shadows.

She dressed in yet another pair of snug, faded jeans and a sweatshirt, then went downstairs, her boots clopping on the wooden stairs. She found all the animals had migrated back down to the large, soft bed. Obviously they didn't care much for the crowded quarters of the small, overstuffed love seat she'd slept on last night.

Robin frowned, just now realizing that her

usually cautious cats seemed to have taken to Patrick right away. She stared at the bed, pondering this surprise. Rosie and Pooh were quite discriminating, and Robin had always considered them fairly good judges of character.

Patrick sighed and shifted position, and Robin suddenly noticed the picture he made. Surrounded by a variety of furred creatures, he looked like a child nesting amid stuffed animals. Her gaze softened, and she shook her head, her eyes lingering on his tousled dark hair. A sudden longing to reach out and smooth back the fallen locks surprised her.

She told herself it was like the feeling she had when she saw a picture of a lion stretched out in the sun, looking soft and sleepy. The urge was there to reach out and touch that velvety warm fur, but she knew that to do so was to risk losing a finger or two. Or her whole hand. Or in this case, she admitted ruefully, her heart.

THREE

Would the man never wake up? When Robin had come downstairs, she had fed the animals, then gone out to the shelter and tended the animals there as well. Patrick continued to sleep soundly when she returned. Shrugging, she fixed breakfast, rattling the pots and pans a little louder than necessary. Still he snored contentedly.

She took his plate over to him, hoping the aromas of warm blueberry muffins and fresh-brewed coffee would penetrate. When that didn't work, she nudged the bed. Not a sound. She nudged it harder. Patrick rolled over onto his back, settling down into a more comfortable position.

He had woken her up in the middle of the night with no apologies, then expected to sleep away half the day? Not on your life, buster! she thought. "Patrick." She poked him in the shoulder. He mumbled and pulled the cover higher around his face.

"Oh no you don't." She poked him again. "Patrick. Wake up."

He muttered something unintelligible, then opened one bleary eye. "What-time-is-it?" He ran the words together so it sounded like one word.

"It's after eight."

He groaned and turned back onto his side. "It's practically the middle of the night. Wake me up in a couple of hours." He snuggled his head down into the pillow.

"Sorry." Robin grabbed the blanket and tugged it down, stopping at his waist—she'd already noticed the jeans lying on the floor next to the bed.

Patrick finally opened the other eye. "I normally sleep until eleven."

"Well, this is not the Shady Rest Hotel, and there is no room service, so I suggest you eat your breakfast now. Otherwise, lunch will be served at my convenience. And," she added, "I may forget about fixing it altogether." Leaving the tray on the nightstand, she left the room.

Patrick levered up on one elbow and watched her walk away. Well, it looked as if Ms.

McKenna-Exbury had decided to be cranky to-day. Shrugging, he yawned and reached for his tray just in time to see the raccoon make off with a slice of fruit. Patrick shook his head. He was getting used to it, he decided. He didn't even blink when Pooh tried to steal a strip of bacon from his plate; he simply held the plate out of reach until the cat got bored with waiting and jumped off the bed.

He heard a muffled laugh and looked up to find Robin watching him from the doorway. "Do you have any pets?" she asked.

What happened to Oscar the Grouch? Patrick eyed her warily and shook his head. "I'm not home enough."

She came over and took his tray, setting it on the counter. "Did you have a pet when you were young?" When he nodded, she said, "Wait, don't tell me. Let me guess."

She tilted her head to one side and stared at him a moment. "A dog, right?"

"Yeah. It was—"

"A big dog. A collie, maybe, or a retriever."

"Wrong."

"Wrong?"

"It was a Yorkshire terrier."

Robin's jaw dropped. "You're not serious. Rosie could eat two dogs that size for lunch."

Patrick grinned. "I used to sneak him into school in my backpack."

This put a whole new light on things, thought Robin. She'd pictured him as having a large, boisterously affectionate, and very active dog—a Frisbee-in-the-park kind of dog. Instead, he'd had a teeny-weeny fluffy ribbons-in-her-ears kind of dog. That didn't fit at all with what she knew about Patrick. "He was a gift, right?"

"Nope, I picked him out myself."

"Why?" She couldn't figure this out.

He shrugged. "I liked the idea of a dog I could sneak into places. I took him to school, to the library, even to church once. I'd zip him up in my jacket, and no one would even know."

Now she could understand it. Still, she'd have given almost anything to see a young Patrick cuddling a dainty little Yorkshire terrier.

When he smiled, Robin couldn't forestall an answering smile. The very idea of his lugging around a cutesy dog like that was ridiculous. Ludicrous. Endearing. Funny, how the sharing of one silly detail could feel so intimate, so special.

She didn't want to feel this way about Patrick. She wanted to be friendly and pleasant but impersonal. Only he wouldn't let her. He teased her, confused her, rattled her. Yet utterly charmed, Robin took the rocking chair next to the bed, and they talked awhile longer before she excused herself to do chores.

Outside, she didn't go immediately to the shelter. Instead, she went for a walk—away from Patrick. Even being in the same room with him muddled her thinking. What was there about this man that seemed to turn her inside out whenever he was around? And when he wasn't?

He was undeniably attractive, but Robin had always considered herself unaffected by outward appearances. After all, she had schooled herself long and hard in it during her year-long marriage— and especially during the fiasco afterward. So why this reaction to this man?

Maybe she and Patrick had known each other in some past life. She toyed briefly with the idea of reincarnation. That would explain her instantaneous reaction to him. What a shame she didn't believe in it.

There was another interesting possibility. Love at first sight. But she didn't believe in that either.

Of course, there was *lust* at first sight. Heaven knew, that applied. And *like* at first sight—well, that was possible. She didn't want to like him, but somehow couldn't *not* like him. Robin sighed and massaged her temples. Shaking her head, she pulled the gloves from her pocket. For now, there were animals to feed, cages to clean, bandages to change.

Robin found one excuse or another to stay busy outside the rest of the day, leaving Patrick to his own devices. She came in only long enough to fix lunch for him and point out a stack of magazines in the corner.

Joey dropped by for a few minutes in the late afternoon to bring a pair of crutches left from his skiing accident the year before. He talked with Patrick briefly, then went around back to the shelter to see Robin. "How's it going?"

"Okay. Have you heard from Marge and Betsy?"

"I talked to them last night. They'll be staying with Marge's mother through the weekend. How's that litter of woodchucks?"

Robin walked by a row of wire cages to a larger one on the end. "I put food in here every afternoon, and it's gone the next morning, so I'm assuming they're all right. They don't come out of that hollow log while I'm around, though. I should be able to release them in a couple of weeks."

"Where's the vixen I sewed up a few days ago?"

"She's right over here." Robin pointed to a

russet-furred creature curled into a tight pillow. She went over and emptied a can of dog food in the food dish, the sound rousing the dozing fox.

"I see the bandage is off," Joey said. "Did that red-pepper trick I told you about keep her from chewing at it?"

"It worked fine. The wildlife center over in the valley is sending someone for her and the does this week sometime."

"Good. Uh, things all right between you and Trick?"

Things were entirely too all right, Robin thought and felt her face burn. "Everything's just fine, Joey." When he didn't respond, she glanced over at him. "What're you grinning at?"

"Oh, nothing. I always figured you and Patrick would get along well." He looked at his watch. "Gotta go. Call me if you need me." He headed toward his car.

"Oh, wait. I'll have that revised proposal for the foundation ready by tomorrow, I think. Were you serious about driving it over to Front Royal to send it Express Mail for me?"

"Sure." Joey waved a hand, still grinning.

Robin frowned as Joey drove off, maneuvering his car around the potholes in the half-mile-long driveway. He certainly had seemed pleased about something when he left.

Supper was quiet, the silence strained rather than companionable. Robin buried her face in a book, and Patrick shuffled through some papers Joey had brought.

"Is that an interesting book?" Patrick asked after a silence lasting fifteen minutes or more.

Robin glanced up. "It's riveting," she said dryly.

Patrick reached across the table and tilted the book up so he could read the title. "*Herbivorous Mammals*. Yeah, it sounds really engrossing."

"So, is what you're working on riveting?" Robin asked politely.

"It's an in-depth article I'm doing for *Washington Today* magazine."

Robin stood and carried her plate to the sink. "Oh? And are you destroying many lives with it?"

"You're a testy little thing today, aren't you?" Patrick said mildly.

Robin had the grace to look embarrassed. "Sorry," she muttered. "I don't mean to keep taking potshots at you."

"But you just don't like or trust reporters. Right?"

She nodded reluctantly. "I've known a few who would do anything for a story, step on anybody and not care if anyone got hurt in the process."

"I won't deny that there are some reporters like that. But there are also some doctors like that, some lawyers like that, some truck drivers like that—"

"I know it, Patrick. It's just that—"

"But I'm not like that."

"Oh, really? Are you an Eagle Scout then? Or maybe you help little old ladies across the street on alternate Wednesdays."

Patrick heard the cynicism in her voice, and knew it was important to him that she realize he was a man, not just a reporter. "Robin, I've never written a story in which I didn't check and re-check my facts. I've always told the truth."

"As you see it."

"Sure, it's as I see it. That's the only way any of us perceive the truth. I do the best I can. And I'm not just a reporter, the same as you're not just a wildlife rehabilitator. I'm also a son, a brother, a grandson, a semi-Catholic—"

Robin was hard-pressed not to smile at that. "How can you be a semi-Catholic?"

"Well, I'm a Catholic when I remember to go to church."

"Me too," Robin admitted ruefully. "Except I'm more of a semi-Methodist, semi-Presbyterian, and semi-Catholic."

"What?"

"There are three churches in town. I alternate among them."

"That's certainly democratic. My youngest brother is a priest."

"Your brother the Father?"

Patrick grinned amiably. "Are you an only child?"

Robin nodded. "I'd always wanted a brother or sister, though. I guess Joey and Marge are like the siblings I never had, and I love Betsy as though she were really my niece. She even calls me Aunt Robin." To her surprise, she was actually enjoying this talk with Patrick.

She shook her head a little, reminding herself that whatever else he was, he was also a reporter. Even if he weren't, she didn't need any distractions right now. Not when she stood to gain so much. Or lose it. Deliberately, she set the book aside and pulled out a stack of papers.

She poised the pencil in her hand, ready to write, and glanced at Patrick. "I hope you don't mind, but I really need to get this finished. It has to go in the mail tomorrow."

Patrick lay on the bed, ostensibly working on his article, but more often than not watching Robin. She worked with single-minded intensity. But though she was silent, she wasn't still. Patrick turned over a paper and noted something on the back, then his gaze swung to her. She wrote furiously, then paused, tapping the pencil in a staccato rhythm on the table. One foot, poised on its toe, swung back and forth in time to the tapping.

He wondered if that restless energy was so integral a part of Robin that she tossed and turned all night, tangling in the covers and waking up sideways in the bed. Or did she cuddle into a little ball and sleep like a log, using the night to recharge?

There were so many mysteries about Robin that he wanted to solve. So many questions he wanted to answer. As a reporter, he'd been trained to ferret out the truth. He could accept no less than that.

Robin was still on Patrick's mind several hours later, as he tried to read. He finally put the magazine down. The puzzle of the intriguing Teresa Exbury/Robin McKenna was far more interesting.

No time like the present to solve it. Patrick cast a quick glance upstairs. The loft had been dark and quiet for quite some time. He hobbled over to the phone in the corner of the kitchen and placed a long-distance call to Bill Marsh, a fellow reporter he sometimes teamed up with.

"This better be good!" a gravelly voice growled into the phone.

"I'm always good," Patrick drawled.

"I should've known it was you," Bill sighed. "You're the only one I know who keeps these hours. What's up?"

"I need a favor and I wanted to make sure I caught you at home."

"At two A.M. I'm not usually out on the town. So spit it out, would you? I know it's the top of the evening for you, but it's the middle of the night for me."

Patrick ran a hand through his hair, suddenly overwhelmed by guilt. Did it really matter if Robin was Teresa or Teresa was Robin? It wasn't any of his business. Still, he rationalized, he didn't intend to actually *do* anything. He only wanted to know the truth about her. She'd never even know. "I'm curious about some background info on somebody."

"Who?"

"Her name is Robin McKenna. I think she used to be known as Teresa Exbury. She's currently a licensed wildlife rehabilitator in Needle Ridge, Virginia."

"You on a story?"

"No, she's a friend. I'm just researching something."

"I'll do what I can. How do I reach you? You at home?"

"Uh, no, I'll be out of town for a few days. I'd better call you. Oh, and could you get in touch with Clay and tell him not to expect me in for another week or two? Thanks, Bill. Sorry I woke you."

"No problem. I was only sleeping."

Patrick set the receiver down and stared uneasily at the phone. After all, Robin was doing him a favor by letting him stay here and, acid-tongued though she might be, she had gentle hands and a warm, contagious smile. Maybe he should call Bill off.

He redialed, but hearing footsteps padding down the stairs, he hurriedly broke the connection after the first ring. Quickly he hung up the receiver and reached for a glass on the kitchen counter.

Robin's eyes blinked against the light, and she frowned at him. "What's going on? I thought I heard you talking to somebody."

"Me?" Patrick's eyes widened, and he held up the glass. "I'm just getting something to drink, only I can't figure out how to work this thing." He indicated the cast-iron pump.

She rolled her eyes and smothered a yawn. "You *are* a city boy, aren't you?"

He gave her a warm, wicked grin. "But I'm a fast learner, Red. A real fast learner. Want to teach me something?"

"Yeah," she grumbled, tearing her gaze away from his face. "Manners. Two nights in a row you've awakened me from a dead sleep. Do you sleep so late in the mornings because you spend all night thinking of ways to keep me up too?"

Patrick's eyes ran over her, reminding Robin that she was naked beneath her flannel gown. "Lady"—his voice lowered to a husky rumble—"I can think of lots of ways to keep you awake at night." His eyes fastened on the rapidly hardening tips of her breasts, barely visible beneath the soft fabric.

Robin stifled an urge to squirm beneath his avid gaze. "So can I," she said, feeling breathless at his intense scrutiny. "But most of them involve boiling oil or Chinese water torture."

"Hey, whatever turns you on."

You do. For a heart-stopping moment, Robin feared she'd said the words out loud. What came out of her mouth was almost as bad. "What turns you on?"

The warm glow in Patrick's eyes heated until it burst into flames. "You want to know what turns me on, Red? I'll tell you. Lying in your bed at night and wondering if you've ever made love under those silly stars overhead. Thinking about you on top of me, with your hair falling around us like a curtain."

Robin stared at him, transfixed. She knew she ought to turn around and go right back upstairs to her safe little bed, but she couldn't seem to tear herself away from his mesmerizing voice.

"And you know what else turns me on? Wondering if you have to lie down to zip those tight jeans you like to wear. Wanting to know if that sharp tongue of yours could be as inventive in bed as it is at spouting insults." His voice lowered to a sensual whisper. "And you know what turns me on most of all? It's knowing that I turn you on too."

"No," Robin breathed.

"Don't lie to me, Red, and don't lie to yourself. Your eyes give you away every time. But even if they didn't, something else would." At her bewildered look, he reached out a lazy finger and traced a circle around an impudent nipple thrusting against her flannel gown.

Robin opened her mouth to speak, but all that came out was a soft moan. Did a cobra's victim feel like this? she wondered hazily. So helpless— limbs languorous and weighted, unable to look away from the hypnotic eyes that moved ever closer?

Her eyes drifted shut as his head moved closer still. She felt his lips brush over hers, the barest touch. But it was enough to leave her lips tingling, hungry for more. She waited for him to continue, but he didn't. When she opened her eyes, she ran her tongue over her bottom lip, tasting Patrick. Then she looked up to meet his sweet-syrup eyes and self-satisfied smile.

"I told you," he murmured.

The spell that had held her in thrall broken, Robin whirled away a few steps, her eyes glittering gold sparks. "In a pig's eye!" she snapped. "Now if you'll excuse me, I need my sleep. You're not the only injured critter I have to baby-sit."

Patrick watched as she stomped away, her bare feet slapping against the wooden floor. So she considered him just another injured critter, did she? He slammed the glass he'd been holding down on the counter.

Suppose she really looked at him as simply one more creature to tend—to feel sorry for? He hated the idea.

But he hadn't imagined that spark of awareness between them. He knew she wanted him— he'd stake his life on it. She was just too damned stubborn to admit it. He'd have to work on that. Occupied with his thoughts, he absently cut off the light and went to bed.

He stared at the gleaming stars on the ceiling and wondered why he needed for her to acknowledge the desire that flared between them. When had it become so important to him that she realize what she felt for him was different from what she felt for the rest of her so-called "critters"?

Patrick turned onto his side, punched his pillow down, and met the disgruntled gaze of a sleepy-eyed raccoon. "So," he murmured with a resigned sigh. "She sees you and me in the same light, huh?" He shook his head at the raccoon. "Well, not if I have anything to say about it." He determinedly closed his eyes and willed sleep to come.

The next morning Robin made an obvious effort to avoid meeting his eyes. Patrick didn't make it easy for her. He followed her around the small kitchen, asking her unnecessary questions. He wondered how long she could go on giving monosyllabic responses.

After a few minutes of this, Robin finally pointed an imperious finger at the table. "Sit," she ordered, and turned back to the stove. Patrick felt a surge of triumph. He was getting to her. At least when she was angry with him, she couldn't lump him with all the cats, raccoons, skunks, and whatever else she had hanging around.

Robin thought getting him out from under foot would help, but it didn't. He sat at the table, his head propped on his hands, and watched her with rapt interest.

"Do you ever wear anything other than jeans and oversize sweaters?"

"No." She peeked in the oven again. She wished those muffins would hurry up and bake. With Patrick's mouth full of food, he couldn't ask her so many questions.

"Why not?"

"Why should I?"

"No reason. Seems a shame to cover that delightful body of yours with yards of excess fabric, that's all."

Robin's hand tightened on the pot holder she held, while she debated on whether throwing it at him would shut him up or merely make things worse. "I dress to please myself, not you."

"You know, now that I think about it, the way you dress is very sexy. A man can't help but wonder what treasures you're hiding under that huge sweater. Of course," he went on casually, "from those tight jeans, I already know you've got long legs and a nice a—" He jumped as Robin slammed two glasses and a pitcher in front of him.

"Make yourself useful," she bit out.

Deciding it would be in his best interests not

to smile, he restrained himself and concentrated on pouring the orange juice. He really wanted to concentrate on her instead—her eyes golden with pique, her hair crackling about her shoulders, her cheeks flushed with anger. *Lump me with the rest of your animals now*, he wanted to shout.

He found himself wondering what color her eyes would be when she made love, wondering if she'd have the same pink flush on her face. A sudden tightening around the seam of his jeans forced him to banish the thoughts.

Patrick shifted position in his chair, hoping it wasn't readily apparent what he'd been thinking. She already knew he was attracted to her; it was probably better, at this point, that she not know how much.

"Here." The pottery plate clattered as Robin set it on the table.

"Thanks."

She set her plate down on the opposite side of the table, picked up her fork, and ate, concentrating on her plate as seriously as if it held the answers to the world's most important questions.

"Tell me something, Robin," he said quietly. "Is it me or the fact that I'm a reporter that you object to the most?"

"I don't know what you're talking about?"

"I think you do."

"I don't think reporters are an especially honest lot, but that has nothing to do with the way I feel about you."

"If that's not it, then tell me what is."

"Patrick, it's nothing. Okay?" She shoved a careless hand through her hair, pushing it off her face. "I want to eat my breakfast in peace. Can't we discuss something innocuous—like the weather?"

With a move that shocked Robin out of her seat, Patrick slammed his fist on the table. "Dammit! I'm not a fool, Robin. I can plainly see the chip on your shoulder. If you were a man, I'd knock it off. But you're not, and if I could get to my feet fast enough to catch you, I'd kiss it off." He took a deep breath and lowered his voice. "Since I can't do either, why don't you save us both a lot of headaches and tell me?"

"What is it you want from me?" Robin turned her palms up entreatingly.

"I want to know why you feel so defensive around me. Is it me or my job?"

She turned away and carried her half-eaten breakfast to the sink. "You keep harping on your job. I've never said I hate your job."

"You haven't had to come right out and say it, Red. It's been obvious enough."

Robin sighed. "Why can't you just let it drop?"

"Because I don't want another replay of yesterday. It was damned chilly around here. Why can't you trust me enough to tell me why you don't like reporters?"

Robin walked over to the table and gripped the back of a chair. "Okay, you wanna know? I think reporters are a bloodthirsty lot who care only for their story and not a whit for the lives that might get destroyed in the process. So, no, I don't trust reporters. And as for trusting you, well, I don't know you well enough to trust you either."

"For God's sake, Robin, tell me something I don't already know!"

"This is going nowhere, Patrick. Absolutely nowhere. And I've got work to do."

It was a shame she wasn't wearing high heels, Patrick thought. The staccato clicking they would have made on the wooden floor as she marched smartly away would have been quite effective.

FOUR

Patrick got to his feet, intending to go after her. One step on his foot, however, and he sank back down. He looked at the raccoon keeping vigil next to the chair, hoping for a spare crumb. "I don't even know what that was all about. For Pete's sake, I've only known the lady for a few days. I shouldn't care whether she trusts me or not." He dropped a corner of toast on the floor for the animal.

Apparently he wasn't the sort of man who inspired trust. Hadn't he learned that the hard way? His own wife hadn't even trusted him. He cradled his head in his hands and allowed the memories to wash over him. Shelly. He'd met her his last year in college and married her right after he graduated.

He'd been enamored of his fragile-looking

blue-eyed, blond wife. He'd been so enamored that he'd overlooked her strange behavior and swallowed every one of her weak excuses. And, of course, his new job as a sports reporter for a local Maryland paper had kept him busy enough that he wasn't always there. Maybe if he'd been around more, he'd have discovered she was an addict. He'd always felt guilty about that, even though her own parents hadn't even known.

If only she had trusted him, had trusted his love enough to tell him the truth, he might have been able to prevent what happened. Instead, her secret had destroyed their marriage—and her.

Patrick straightened his shoulders and stood. He shook the image away—after all, that had been eight years ago. Hell, it had been a lifetime ago. Since then, his motto had been "Travel often, travel light." If he ever got involved again, it would be with a woman who trusted him heart and soul. However, he didn't intend to get involved—especially not with a redheaded vixen who had an animal fetish.

He'd be out of this isolated backwoods in a day or two, and he and Robin would never see each other again. It shouldn't bother him at all that she didn't trust him as far as she could throw him. So why did it?

Patrick shook his head. He couldn't bear the

thought of staring at these same four walls again today. He limped over to the bed and grabbed the crutches Joey had left propped there. It took only a few minutes of lurching around the kitchen before he steadied enough to maneuver without danger of falling.

He went to the door and stuck his head out. It was unseasonably cool today, so he dug an old college sweatshirt out of his suitcase. He pulled it on and lurched awkwardly outside, looking for Robin.

The structure attached to the side of the house looked like an enclosed carport. Small windows had been stuck in with no rhyme or reason— wherever the builder had wanted to let in a little light, but before Patrick peeked in, he walked to the back where a tall wooden fence enclosed an area that looked to be several hundred square feet.

If he stood on tiptoes, he could just see over the fence. Two deer, both with bandaged legs, stood in one corner, grazing contentedly in the dappled shade of a barely leafed-out dogwood. A fox sunned in a portable cage in the opposite corner, while the skunk—he assumed it was the same one he'd seen sunning on the kitchen table—had curled up in a sunny spot in the middle. Several animals he couldn't identify had curled into furry brown pillows next to the house.

"What are you doing up?" Robin's voice came from just behind him.

Patrick turned. "I'm doing you a favor."

She crossed her arms and raised her eyebrows. "And what's that?"

"I'm saving you the trouble of explaining to the coroner how a perfectly healthy man died of boredom."

Patrick could tell Robin didn't want to smile by the way she fought the one tugging at the corners of her mouth. "Well, come on," she said reluctantly, "and I'll give you the grand tour." She led the way into the attached enclosure.

Patrick looked around curiously. Double rows of cages lined the walls of the room. Larger cages formed another row down the middle. About half of them were empty, and he commented on this.

"Give me another month and most of them will be full," remarked Robin. "We're a bit early in the breeding season to have too many young ones. Just an early litter of woodchucks and a few rabbits and lots of squirrels—squirrels usually have their first litter in February or March."

She pointed out a full-grown possum eyeing them from the corner of its cage. "I got her a few days ago. She was hit by a car, but doesn't seem to be too badly injured. I'll be releasing her in a couple of days." She walked over to a cage where her raccoon was staring down another one. "Shoo!" She waved her hand, and Tripod jumped off the counter.

Patrick's gaze followed him as he ran outside in his odd three-legged gait. "How did he lose his leg?"

Robin set her jaw. "Steel trap. It broke his leg in two places. A kid in town found him and rescued him, but infection set in, and Joey had to take the leg."

"They don't have laws about those traps?"

She shook her head. "About the only law I know of is one requiring them to be checked once a day. But I know the game wardens around here are too busy with poachers to see that they are."

"You'd think they would have come up with a more humane alternative by now," Patrick grimaced.

"I'm not sure I even believe in man's humaneness anymore. Not when I see such shining examples of man inhumanity."

Patrick eyed her curiously. "You don't believe in man's humaneness. You don't believe in reporters. What else do you not believe in?"

Robin gave a sudden impish grin. "Well, I don't believe in eating turnips or brussels sprouts.

I don't believe in rainy Independence Days, and I don't believe in giving socks or underwear for Christmas."

"What about Santa Claus, the Tooth Fairy, and the Easter Bunny?"

"What about them?"

"You don't believe in those."

"Who says I don't?"

"Do you?"

"Sure. I also believe in the man in the moon and little green apples."

Robin leaned against an empty cage and crossed her arms, staring down at the scuffed toes of her tennis shoes. "I don't know. Maybe it's easier to believe in fantasy than reality. I mean, I'd like to believe in truth, but I'm not sure I can. I could say I don't believe in lies and broken hearts, but they happen too. So, how about you, Patrick? What do you *not* believe in?"

Patrick appeared to give the matter serious thought. "I don't believe in pizza without beer or Thanksgiving without turkey and—" He looked straight at her. "I do believe in truth, because without it lies and broken hearts happen, and I don't believe in them. I don't believe in secrets either."

Turning abruptly, Robin opened a door leading out into the fenced area. "This is where some

of the more ambulatory animals can roam around."
She indicated what looked like a large doghouse.
"That's where Chanel and Tripod usually stay."

"So they don't always sleep in the bed?"

"Almost never."

Patrick pointed at a child's plastic swimming
pool propped up against the house. "What do you
use that for?"

"For the occasional duck. Usually it's just
Ritz, though."

"Ritz? The mallard who likes showers?"

"That's him."

"Why on earth do you call him Ritz?"

"His full name is Ritz Quackers." Robin said
sheepishly.

Patrick let out a full-throated laugh. Robin
could only stare wistfully. It had been a long time
since she had laughed so uninhibitedly. There
had been little enough reason to laugh during her
brief marriage, and even less afterward.

As a wife, she had spent most of her time
trying desperately to believe the many lies her
husband told her. After his death, she should have
been able to square her shoulders and get on with
her life. Instead, she'd had to deal with whispers
accusing her of complicity, of guilt.

The most damaging whispers, the ones that
had cost her a job and most of her friends, had

been those of the reporters. And though she knew in her head that Patrick hadn't even been there, it didn't seem to make any difference to her heart. It still circled Patrick as warily as a dog circling a stranger.

"Robin?"

"Hmm?"

"You looked a million miles away there for a minute."

No, she thought, just about five years and a couple of hundred miles away. "Oh, sorry. Just daydreaming, I guess." She went back inside and began fumbling with a water jug.

Patrick stood just inside the door, watching every move she made. Robin began to fidget uncomfortably. To her horror, she found herself wishing she had worn newer jeans and the pink sweater she'd bought in Front Royal last fall.

Would he never leave? Maybe she could hurry him along a little. "Well, I have some work to do. If you want to go back inside, I have some books upstairs I can bring down."

"More on animals?"

"No, I have some others too."

"Thanks. I'll take you up on that."

Robin felt like breathing a sigh of relief but restrained herself.

"I'll get them later, though. Right now, I'd like to help you."

"Help me?" Robin cringed when her voice squeaked. "I thought Dr. Martin told you to keep that ankle propped up."

"He said to elevate it *most* of the time. I've had it propped up all night—an hour or two hobbling on it this morning isn't going to hurt." Patrick leaned one of his crutches against the wall. "So what can I do?"

Leave me alone, Robin thought. Instead, she pointed to the bag on the floor. "You can put a handful of that kibble in the raccoon's cage, as well as the possum's. Then put some in the bowl right outside the back door for the woodchucks." As he turned to get the kibble, she added, "Don't try to touch them. They'll bite."

"And after I'm finished?"

"You could check the cages for fresh water." Robin stepped over to the table and began filling a syringe with a white liquid.

"What's that?" Patrick asked.

"It's puppy formula."

"Puppy formula?"

"It's what I feed the baby squirrels."

"Where are they?"

"Over here." She lifted the door on a cage next to the table, then pulled back a loose covering of soft terry cloth to reveal four tiny pink creatures, covered with a soft gray fuzz. She reached in and lifted one, holding it close while she fed it.

Patrick, in the midst of dishing out kibble, stopped and watched her, enchanted at the soft green shade of her eyes as she cooed at the baby animal. Patrick imagined she'd sound the same cooing at a baby. He closed his eyes and could almost see the baby—a tiny bundle with the softest red-gold fuzz on her head, and little arms and legs moving nonstop.

When he opened his eyes, he saw Robin's tender smile, and a sudden pang hit him. He wanted her to smile at him that way. He wanted to taste that smile, run his tongue around it. He wanted to feel her smile when she kissed him back.

With a sigh, he turned away and distributed the food and water. "Anything else I can do? Do you want me to feed that one?"

Robin tucked the last baby back into the terry cloth nest and turned around. "You mean him?" She pointed to the half-covered cage in the corner. "He's a barn owl. He's nocturnal, so I'll feed him tonight. You can check the heating pads in those three cages there and make sure they're all on low."

"What do you use the heating pads for?" he asked as he checked the indicators.

"Baby mammals don't always generate a lot of body heat. This keeps them warm."

"And what keeps you warm?" His voice held the mild roughness of finely grained sandpaper.

Robin snapped her head around to find Patrick standing right behind her. She backed away a little. "Um, thanks for helping me," she stammered. "I'll go bring a couple of books down for you. Do you like mysteries, science fiction?"

Patrick didn't budge. "I'd love to volunteer."

"To get the books?"

"To keep you warm."

"I manage quite well," Robin said primly. Why didn't he move? She inched back a little more, only this time he stepped forward. He stood so close now that she could feel the warmth radiating from him. "I really ought to finish my chores . . ." Her voice trailed off lamely as he reached out and smoothed back her hair, his hand lingering as if he couldn't bear to pull it away.

"This is quite a job you have, Red, taking care of all these animals. Lots of long hours, hard, solitary work," Patrick murmured. "Who takes care of you?"

"No one. I mean, I take care of myself." She wanted to put more physical distance between them, but somehow she couldn't make her feet move.

His hand stroked her hair one more time, then cupped her chin. "And a fine job you do of that too." His thumb traced her bottom lip. "Smile for me, Robin," he urged, his voice as smooth as sun-warmed honey. "Please, just one smile."

She complied, shyly, hesitantly. Patrick slid his hand behind her neck and immediately bent his head to taste it. His lips moved over hers, slick and sweet and hot, wooing her to trust. When her lips softened and parted, he ran his tongue over them before hungrily slipping between.

Her tongue answered his, and he moaned and savored the unbearable rightness of it. Dimly, he realized he needed to breathe sometime, but he needed this more. He tore his lips from hers only long enough to draw in a ragged breath before claiming them again, rediscovering their rich secrets.

Her kisses were headier than the strongest wine, and Patrick wanted more. He leaned forward to pull her closer to him but put too much weight on his injured ankle. A sharp stab of pain shot clear up to his knee, and he stumbled back. Grabbing on to the edge of the table, he muttered an oath.

"Are you all right?" Robin's voice sounded muffled.

"Yeah, I'm okay." Patrick gritted his teeth as the pain subsided, then smiled at her. "You made me forget I'm not quite ready for the Olympics yet." His gaze lingered on her. Her eyes were luminous and hazy, her cheeks flushed rose, and her lips still red and moist from the pressure of his. He reached out a hand to caress her, but she stepped back.

"I don't think that's a good idea," she said faintly.

"Maybe I do."

Her voice was stronger now. "But a kiss has to be mutual—"

Patrick gave a lopsided smile. "Red, that kiss was about as mutual as you can get. You can't pretend it didn't happen."

Robin took a deep breath. "I'm not going to. But it won't happen again. I'm not going to get involved with anyone right now. In any way." She turned away and began fiddling with one of the cages. "I think you should go back in and get off that ankle. There's ice in the freezer if you need to pack it. I'll be in shortly to fix lunch."

"Won't happen again, huh?" Patrick muttered as he hobbled away. "Not going to get involved? We'll see about that."

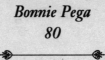

Joey came by after lunch. He looked at a couple of animals for Robin, then went inside to talk to Patrick. "How's the ankle, Trick?"

"Not too bad, as long as I don't try to mambo. How're things at the clinic?"

"Fine. Susan Cogbill's coming back from vacation two days early, so I'll have off tomorrow, as well as the day after. I can pick you up after hours tonight and take you back with me."

Patrick could think of nothing he wanted to hear less than that. He didn't know what was happening between him and Robin, but he didn't want to leave until he'd found out. He never backed down from a challenge. Especially a challenge with strawberry hair and changeable hazel eyes. "Uh, no, Joey. I don't think that would be a good idea."

Joey stared at Patrick. "What do you mean?"

"You've worked double shifts eight days straight. You need to catch up on your sleep and your chores. I'm sure Marge left you a list."

"Well, that's true, but it really wouldn't be any trouble to—"

"No, no, I wouldn't hear of it. I'm fine where I am."

"Well," Joey said slowly, "I do feel like I

could sleep about twenty-four hours. Are you sure it'll be okay with Robin? She's not used to having anybody underfoot—at least not two-legged anybodies."

"Oh, I'm sure it'll be fine with her."

"I'd better check with her before I go." Joey got up to leave.

"Uh, Joey? I wish you wouldn't do that."

Joey turned and leaned against the edge of the table, a look of dawning interest on his face. "Why is that?"

"I wish you wouldn't, that's all. Now what's that look for?" he asked, as his friend's face lit up.

"Nothing." Joey headed out the door. "Your secret's safe with me," he called over his shoulder.

"Yeah," Patrick muttered. "Safe with you and everyone else in earshot."

He heard Robin corner Joey right outside. "What secret's safe with you?"

"Oh, that's a private joke between Trick and me."

"I've been meaning to ask you. How'd he ever get the nickname Trick? Was it only because it's short for Patrick?"

Joey laughed. "He earned every letter of that name in college. He was the top practical joker on campus."

"Really?" Patrick could swear he heard something that sounded like satisfaction in her voice. "Tell me more."

Spare me, thought Patrick.

"You'll have to ask Trick to tell you sometime. I need to get these figures in the mail for you, grab a bite, and head back to the clinic to cover Susan's four-to-seven shift."

"Thanks a lot for mailing it overnight for me. I know this has been a grueling schedule for you. When does Susan come back?"

Patrick listened intently. He hoped Joey was a good liar.

"Well, she's not scheduled for a few days yet. By the way, when does the center come to pick up the fox and those two does?"

"Sometime this week. They weren't specific. Thanks again for mailing that. See you later."

Patrick breathed a sigh of relief. Safe for a day or two longer.

"Which of your secrets is safe with Joey?" Robin asked from the doorway.

"Which one isn't?" Patrick shrugged lightly. "When you go to college with somebody, you're bound to rack up a few."

"Sounds like you racked up more than most," Robin said dryly.

"So where'd you go to college, Red?" He'd

rather change the subject. He didn't care much for the idea of Robin hearing about his youthful misadventures.

"Radcliffe."

Patrick smiled and nodded. He'd known it. Her breeding and education showed. "I didn't know they taught courses there in wild-animal care."

"They don't. I learned the hard way." Robin went upstairs. She reappeared a couple of minutes later and tossed a couple of books on the bed. "I hope these are all right."

Patrick looked at them. One was a current best-selling spy thriller, the other an Agatha Christie mystery. "They're fine." He watched as Robin pulled on gloves and tugged a wide-brimmed hat on her head. "Where're you going? Can I help you do something?"

"I'm going to go weed the peas and kale, then till some manure into the rest of the garden area. I can manage it myself." Robin went to the door, then turned back to Patrick. Can I get you anything else before I go out?"

"No." Patrick stared at her. Silhouetted with the sun behind her, in her wide-brimmed hat she suddenly looked like one of those picture-book brides. His imagination took it one step further and added a bouquet of flowers and a white lace gown. Hell, no!

"Excuse me?"

"Uh, I said I don't need anything else."

Robin shrugged and went out, leaving Patrick to struggle with the picture in his mind. He couldn't handle that lace dress and the flowers. But, hell, he was a writer. He could rewrite the scenario, couldn't he? Suppose he pitched the flowers or, better yet, replaced the bouquet with a bunch of red roses stuffed in a vase?

Patrick folded his arms behind his head and took the scene further. He'd place the vase on a table, next to a silver ice bucket chilling a very good wine. And he'd place the table with the roses and wine in a room with a glowing fireplace and lots of pillows. Robin would be there, but instead of a wedding dress, she'd be wearing black lace. Very little of it. He smiled. He liked this fantasy much better.

The mattress bounced when one of the cats—he could never remember which was which—jumped on it, and he frowned at the interruption. Well, it was better to shelve his fantasies. After all, "Travel often, travel light."

Funny, he hadn't been doing that the past few days, and didn't miss it a bit. Worse yet, the idea didn't hold near the appeal it used to. Strange how sharing this cabin with prickly, obstinate Robin seemed more like being at home than when he was alone in his upscale Georgetown apartment. He didn't like that train of thought either, so he hastily picked up one of the books.

He thumbed through the Agatha Christie novel, but he'd read it before, and he put down the spy novel after reading the first few pages. There were secrets enough to think about right now without reading a book about them. He ended up taking *Small Mammal Care* from the nightstand and finishing the chapter on baby squirrels.

After an hour or two, he put the book down and swung his feet off the bed. He hated feeling confined. He was used to being on the go from the time he got up until he went to bed. He grabbed his crutches and roamed restlessly around the downstairs.

Looking out the small window over the kitchen sink, Patrick saw Robin at a distance on her hands and knees in her garden. With that hat on her head and the light breeze wisping her hair across her face, she looked as innocent as a young girl. However, he knew she had the cynical edge of a woman who'd been hurt. No doubt it had happened in that other life of hers—the one she didn't trust him enough to tell him about.

He sat at the table and tried to work on his article, but couldn't drum up any enthusiasm for it. He'd rather be out in the garden with Robin. An impatient hand dug through his hair. Maybe Robin's restlessness was contagious.

A loud thump from overhead drew him out of his chair. He hobbled over to the steps and peered up, but couldn't see anything. Grabbing hold of the handrail, he managed to climb the stairs without putting too much weight on his ankle. As soon as he reached the top, he saw the reason for the noise. An overturned vase lay on the floor, and one of the cats sat sniffing at the mangled flowers.

He stuffed the flowers back in the cut-glass vase and wiped the moisture from the bottom with his hand before setting it back on the dresser. He glanced around the room and shook his head. The downstairs was much bigger and austere, while the upstairs swung in the other direction.

There was an overstuffed floral print sofa against one wall with a rose satin-and-lace comforter folded across one end. Floor-to-ceiling shelves housed hundreds of books, as well as a television set, a VCR, and a selection of almost any other electronic toy he could think of. A thick mauve carpet covered the floor, and sunlight streamed in the two skylights overhead. Robin might eat and sleep downstairs, but she obviously *lived* up here.

Patrick grinned to himself. This room told him a lot about her. He began to realize that the sensuality he'd sensed all along was a very important part of her. This whole room reeked of it. It was all warm colors and soft textures. And regardless of the jeans and bulky sweaters she usually wore, the satin-and-lace comforter as well as the scrap of pink he saw lying on the dresser told him there was a decidedly feminine side to her.

He couldn't keep his hand from snaring the scrap of pink fabric. It was a camisole—the daintiest of satin confections. He revised his earlier fantasy to include pink satin instead of black lace as he rubbed the smooth fabric back and forth between his fingers.

FIVE

"What on God's green earth do you think you're doing?" Robin was aghast to find Patrick in her private sanctuary at all, but especially with a piece of her lingerie clutched in his hand.

Wearing a shameless grin, Patrick turned and held the dainty camisole suspended between thumbs and forefingers. His eyes swung from it to her and back, as if measuring it for size.

"Gimme that!" Robin snatched it out of his hand and tossed it back on the dresser. "You think you can just go snooping anywhere you please. Well, you can't!" She wagged a finger in his face. "This is my personal territory. You stay downstairs. Have you no respect for anyone's privacy? You can't just—"

Her voice broke off suddenly, when Patrick grasped the finger pointing at him and planted a kiss on the end of it. "I wasn't snooping," he said mildly.

She snatched her finger out of his grasp. "What would you call it?"

He cast a sidelong glance at the pink satin puddle on the dresser. "You mean besides admiring the view? I heard a loud noise and came up here to investigate."

"Right." Robin gave a disbelieving snort. "Likely story."

Patrick spread his hands in a gesture of innocence and indicated the wet spot on the floor where the vase had fallen. "I found that vase on the floor, flowers all over the place, and your orange cat sitting next to it."

"Oh." Robin bit her lip. Apparently he *had* heard something. This wasn't the first time that Rosie had tried to play with the flowers in the vase. Still, the thought of him in her special sanctuary made her uncomfortable. There was too much of her in this room. "But why were you—um . . ." Her voice trailed to a halt.

"Fondling?" Patrick supplied, a glint of humor in his eyes.

"Yes. Why were you fondling my . . . my . . ."

"Underwear?"

She took a deep breath and snapped. "Just go back downstairs."

Not only did Patrick not go downstairs, he leaned comfortably back against the dresser. "You know, this is a really nice room. It's warm and homey-looking. You obviously spend most of your time up here. I like the skylights. Did you have those put in, or did they come with the place?"

"They came with it," Robin said shortly.

"How about the built-in bookshelves?"

"I had those put there."

Patrick eyed her for a moment, then crossed his arms and pursed his lips. "You know I've been pacing the floor downstairs half out of my head with boredom. And all this time, up here, you've got enough grown-up toys to keep ten adults busy."

Robin had never thought about that. At least not consciously. However, she was willing to admit that maybe subconsciously she had known he was bored and hoped he'd go away.

"I didn't exactly do it on purpose," she said lamely. "I just didn't think."

"And now?"

She sighed and waved a hand. "Feel free. Read all the books you want, put on some music, watch TV, although the reception isn't great. Just stop playing with my underthings."

He gave her a cocky grin. "I'm curious, Red. Which drawer do you keep your lacies in, anyway?"

She felt the heat begin at her breasts and spread upward. She longed to put her cool palms to her cheeks, but she refused to let him get the best of her, so she jerked open a drawer and waved a hand at it with a flourish. "There. How long have you had this fetish for women's undies, anyway?"

"Let me think." His eyes narrowed as he blatantly ran his gaze over her. "Since a little less than a week ago. As a matter of fact, I seem to have a fetish only about the underwear of hazel-eyed redheads."

When she hastily averted her eyes, he looked down at the open drawer. It was a jumble of soft pastels, lace, satin bows, and embroidered flowers. Nothing blatantly sexy like black garters or sheer teddies. Instead, the garments were all so supremely feminine, it took his breath away.

He knew he was venturing into dangerous territory here. This closet femininity was far more appealing—and erotic—than an overt display would have been. He found himself wondering just what she wore under her serviceable jeans and sweater. Blue lace? Pink satin? Mint-green silk? At his unmistakable physical reaction to those thoughts, he angled his body away from her.

"Happy now?" Robin shut the drawer. "Look, I need to get back out—" She broke off when the phone rang and dashed downstairs to grab it. After a few minutes she called out, "Patrick, they need you down at the sheriff's office to identify the guy who stole your wallet."

She watched to make sure he didn't fall as he carefully made his way down the stairs. Even on crutches, he still had a lithe agility and a certain insolent grace to his movements. When he was safely at the bottom of the stairs, she stepped into the bathroom to make a few quick repairs, leaving the door open.

She was struggling to drag a brush through her tangled hair when Patrick stepped up behind her.

"Let me." Before she could say a word, he took the brush from her hand and began drawing it through her hair. His strokes were slow and sure as he gently worked the brush through the tangles. He ran his free hand over her hair, smoothing it into place.

Robin stared at his reflection, watching his intent expression. When he looked up, his gaze met hers in the mirror, and his hands stilled. Slowly he laid the brush beside the sink, then, holding her gaze, he threaded his fingers through the silky strands.

At the sight of his large hands wound sinuously through her hair, Robin swallowed hard. When he brought a handful of hair up to her face to inhale the fragrance, she tried in vain to moisten her suddenly dry lips. "I, ah, we'd better go. They'll be waiting for you."

Patrick ran his hands over her hair one last time to smooth it, then stepped back, his eyes assuring her this was only a temporary reprieve. He grabbed his crutches and obediently followed her around back to the cherry-red Jeep. Laying the crutches in the back, he climbed in beside her. "Do you need to check the animals before we go? Will they be okay?"

A part of her melted just a little at his real concern. "They've got a good two hours before the next feeding," Robin assured him as she headed down the bumpy driveway. "Baby mammals generally get fed every three or four hours, like a human baby. The adults are fed only once a day, unless they come in really malnourished or dehydrated."

"When you feed the baby squirrels, do you have trouble with them aspirating the formula?"

Robin glanced at Patrick with a question in her eyes. How did he know that certain baby animals accidentally inhale their formula?

Patrick shrugged. "I've been reading. Do you have a problem with feeding them?"

"Sometimes. I just have to take it slow and only feed them a few drops at a time. The same with baby rabbits. It's usually trying to feed them too fast that causes problems."

"How do you make sure they eliminate on schedule? The book said that can be a problem without proper stimulation."

Robin cast another glance at Patrick. She couldn't believe he wanted to discuss the bladder and bowel habits of young rodents, but he seemed genuinely interested. She patiently explained the procedure.

When they passed a two-story brick building, Patrick asked about it. "Oh, that's where Betsy goes to school." There were five or six school buses parked in front waiting for the onslaught of enthusiastic kids who would be pouring out the door any minute.

"So that's the junior high."

"No, that's *the* school. They don't have enough kids to separate them. As it is, there are only about three hundred students total."

"You're kidding! Shoot, I had nearly five hundred in my senior class alone."

"Welcome to Small Town America. This is where if you don't show up at church on Sunday morning, everybody in town knows why by Sunday night. There's not a kinder or nosier bunch of people anywhere in the U.S. Why, I'll bet that the person they picked up with your wallet went to school with the sheriff. And if not the sheriff—"

Patrick broke in, "The deputy." They both laughed.

"Hasn't Joey ever taken you into town on your visits?" Robin asked.

"No. I usually drop in only for a day or two en route somewhere else."

"Well then, I'll give you the grand tour."

"Are you sure we have time?"

"We have all the time in the world," Robin said dryly. "Believe me, it won't take long to see it all. There's Redeemer Presbyterian Church over there. The church across the street is Main Street Methodist, and next door to that is St. Mark's Catholic."

"What do they call this section of town? The holy corner?"

Robin grinned. "Now here's the brand-new shopping center. It actually has a department store, a bookstore, a farm-supply store, a movie theater, a bowling alley, and four—count 'em, four—restaurants."

"Whoa! Big time, huh?"

"Oh, yeah. There's even a video-rental store, complete with game room with eight video games, four pinball games, and a pool table."

"Will wonders never cease?" Patrick murmured. "What's that?" He pointed at a row of holly trees.

"That's our pride and joy. That's Needle Pine Park. The school kids raised money for two years to buy the holly trees; the Methodist church donated the swing sets; and the local garden club took up door-to-door donations to buy the fountain." Robin couldn't hold back a grin at Patrick's bemused look. She figured he'd probably never even been in another town this size. She hadn't either, until she moved here. Now she didn't think she could ever live anywhere else.

Patrick shifted in his seat to look at her as she pulled into a small parking lot next to an unimpressive building. "You really love it here, don't you?"

She nodded. "Yeah. I really do."

"Why?"

Robin paused for a moment. She'd never stopped to ask herself that question. "There's a simple honesty in a small town. Everybody takes you at face value. And in a town this size, if you don't exactly know everybody, you at least know of them."

She removed her keys from the ignition and toyed with the wooden teddy bear attached to the key ring. Her voice was pensive. "They judge you more on contributions you make to the community, less on who you're related to, or how much money your family has." She smiled a little. "And they bring you brownies when you move in and casseroles when you're ill, and they'll shovel your sidewalk when it snows. Without charging you."

"You know," Patrick said, his brow creased in thought, "for a woman who doesn't believe in trust, you sound exactly like you trust them."

Robin stared at him for a moment. He was right; she just hadn't realized it before. "I guess I do," she said slowly. "As much as I can trust anybody." She shook her head. "We'd better go in. They're waiting."

Patrick noticed that almost everybody they passed in the hall knew and spoke to Robin. A round-faced young mother with two toddlers even pressed a ten-dollar bill in Robin's hand before hurrying off after one of the children. He raised an eyebrow.

"She brought me a nest with two baby sparrows last year."

"You're obviously very popular here."

"They seem to appreciate what I do. I've given talks at the school. I've talked to the local garden club and the civic club and the senior citizens' group at the Methodist church. They're fairly environmentally conscious, and they have a lot of what some people would call bleeding hearts."

"What do you call them?"

"Friends. I get donations of fruits or vegetables every week from the two grocery stores. The farm-supply store lets me purchase feed, like kibble, wholesale. Some of the local kids take turns every week or two to animal-sit so I can run errands or even do something really decadent like go to a movie." She stopped in front of a door marked SHERIFF. "What more can I ask?"

What more, indeed? he thought as Robin introduced him to Earl Greene, the tall, sandy-haired deputy. It didn't take long for Patrick to identify his wallet—missing the two hundred dollars he'd had. He was able to identify by photograph the man who'd taken it. The deputy hadn't gone to school with him—he'd gone to school with his brother. When Robin winked at Patrick, he kept from smiling with difficulty.

Patrick was quick to notice that the deputy was interested in Robin. Watching them out of the corner of his eye, Patrick saw that Earl held her hand a lot longer than was necessary. And even when he addressed his remarks to Patrick, he kept his eyes fastened on Robin.

Patrick didn't like it. He liked it even less when Earl called Robin aside, took her hands, and murmured something to her. Robin shook her head and made a soft reply. Patrick strained to hear, but couldn't over the country music emanating from the radio on the desk.

The deputy smiled and said something else. Robin smiled back. At that, Patrick hobbled over to them and placed a possessive hand at Robin's waist. When her eyes widened in surprise, he said, "We'd better be going, Red." He swung a steely gaze to Earl and held out a hand. "Nice to meet you, Deputy." Patrick gripped Earl's hand a little harder than convention dictated, then all but herded Robin out the door.

"What was that all about?" Robin asked breathlessly as she tried to keep up with Patrick. For a man with a sprained ankle, he could sure make tracks on his crutches.

"We don't want to leave the animals too long." He opened Robin's door for her, giving her a flinty smile when she looked at him.

"They'll be fine, I'm sure," she murmured, puzzled. "Why, we even have enough time to run by the grocery store." She pulled out her keys and scrambled in behind the wheel. "Patrick—" He shut the door and hobbled around to the other side. As soon as he'd climbed in, she began again. "Patrick, what in the world's got your goat?"

"Nothing at all," he muttered. "I just love standing around on an injured ankle while Dudley Do-Right drools all over your boots."

"Dudley Do—you mean Earl?"

"Let's go, huh? I have no desire to discuss that backwoods Don Juan."

"Backwoods Don Juan? Patrick—"

"Robin. You talk too much." With no warning, he turned and pulled her to him, crushing his mouth down over hers. His lips were hard, possessive, darkly seductive. His tongue was a silken invader that stormed in to conquer the sweet, slick interior of her mouth. A low groan rumbled in his throat as his hands splayed over her back, urging her body closer to his.

Robin resisted Patrick's sensual onslaught for a moment. She told herself that this was only going to complicate things. But then she couldn't stop her lips from softening beneath his. And she couldn't stop her tongue from answering his challenge. And she couldn't stop her breasts from nestling against the hard muscles of his chest or her fingers from fastening imperiously onto his shoulders and urging him closer still.

When Patrick slid his hands beneath her sweater and smoothed them over the soft skin of her back, Robin caught her breath in a shuddering gasp. She turned slightly to get even closer and banged her knee. Jerking back, she glanced down to see she'd hit the gear shift. Only then did she look up and remember they were still in her Jeep in the parking lot of the Needle Ridge Municipal Offices.

Robin turned away and fumbled with the key in the ignition. She wasn't sure who was breathing harder, her or Patrick, but the Jeep fairly vibrated. Her hands shook as she tried to get the gear shift out of neutral. When she finally did, she avoided looking at Patrick as she pulled out of the parking lot.

"As long as we're here, I thought I'd run by the grocery store." Robin was pleased at the normal sound of her voice. Hopefully, Patrick wouldn't guess that her heart was beating like a jackhammer. "It shouldn't take long. When I did my grocery shopping last week, I didn't know I'd have a houseguest."

Houseguest. So, he'd moved up from critter to houseguest, Patrick thought. How long would it be before she let him graduate to something else? He didn't know how much longer he'd be here, but he hoped it would be long enough. He knew they'd be dynamite together. Just look at the sparks they had set off with a simple kiss. His knees were still shaky.

However, before she'd promote him to lover, he knew he'd have to win her trust. And he wasn't sure how to do that. Or even if it could be done. He wished he knew just what kind of emotional damage she'd endured in the mysterious past she'd apparently turned her back on. Had the loss of her husband been so painful that she'd carried the scars all this time?

Patrick still puzzled over this as he trailed behind Robin at the grocery store. He followed her up one aisle and down another, watching as she loaded up her cart. When she stopped to poke and prod at the produce, it suddenly hit him how domestic it seemed. She could easily be a young wife and mother carefully selecting the ripest fruit for her family. And he? He could be the enamored husband, not wanting to let his beautiful spouse out of his sight.

No, not husband. Patrick shook the thought away. "Travel often, travel light."

"Hmm? Did you say something?" Robin peered over her shoulder at him.

"Huh? Oh, no. No, I didn't."

"I could've sworn I heard something about travel."

"No." Patrick grabbed a head of romaine lettuce. "What I said was 'Friends, Romaines, and Countrymen.'"

"Lettuce have that." Robin grabbed the vegetable out of his hand.

"Lend me an ear?" Patrick waved an ear of corn at her.

Robin just laughed and headed to the checkout. He was a nut, she found herself thinking fondly. She couldn't help but like him. A lot. Maybe it wouldn't hurt to relax a little. He was a reporter, true, but he couldn't possibly know she was anything other than what she seemed. He was pleasant and charming and had a witty offbeat sense of humor. He'd be with her only another couple of days, so why not have fun? She wondered if he liked to play gin rummy.

They loaded the groceries in the backseat of the Jeep—four bags of hers, one bag of free produce from Irwyn, the owner. Robin kissed him on the cheek when he slipped a check from the local Masonic lodge into her hand and told her to use it for a new overhead fan in her shelter.

"Another conquest of yours?" Patrick said sourly, as she pulled out onto the street.

"What?"

"From Dudley Do-Right to the local grocer,

you have most of the men in town wrapped around your finger, don't you?"

She flashed him a brittle smile. "Certainly. I have so many men wanting to go out with me that I have to make them take a number." Robin didn't know what was going on in Patrick's head right now, but if he didn't watch it, she was going to kick him. Good and hard.

"If I wanted to get in line, what number would I have to take?" Patrick asked lightly.

"Ninety-nine!" She reached over and turned on the radio, adjusting the volume a little louder than usual. Perhaps if she made it difficult for him to talk over it, he'd shut up for a while. So much for relaxing around Patrick. He seemed determined to keep her rattled, as if he enjoyed it.

They silently listened to the local news. The announcer read a statement from the mayor calling for a town meeting to discuss the recent crime wave. It seemed there had been one mugging—Patrick's—four incidences of vandalized mailboxes, and two obscene phone calls.

Robin couldn't help but glance at Patrick to see his reaction. He rolled his eyes, but said nothing. Humming to herself, she paid scant attention to the rest of the news, until a name caught her attention. Exbury.

". . . brother of deceased John Douglas Exbury will be extradited by week's end to face felony charges stemming from their smuggling operation. Now in other news . . ." Robin's hands tightened on the steering wheel, and the thundering of her heartbeat in her ears drowned out all other sounds.

Malcolm had been smarter than John Douglas, Robin thought distractedly, because he'd managed to evade the police for several years. John Douglas must have doubted his own ability to do so, because he took the easy way out. If you could call suicide that.

She felt a touch on her arm and glanced down in surprise. Patrick's hand.

"Robin, are you all right?"

Her mouth felt unbearably dry, but she managed to croak out, "What?" She automatically turned her gaze back to the road.

"I asked if you were all right. You look pale. Are you ill?"

"Everything's fine. I just don't feel very well. I'll go lie down for a little while when I get home."

"Do you want me to drive?" His voice was husky with concern.

She somehow forced the corners of her mouth up. "I'll be fine, Patrick."

Thank heaven, she'd driven this route countless times, she thought, because it was surely automatic pilot that was getting her home now. The minute she pulled up in her driveway, she got out of the car and ran into the house, afraid she'd disgrace herself by getting sick in front of Patrick.

She trembled so hard, it was difficult to make it up the stairs. But she did and collapsed on the sofa, huddling into a ball. She drew the comforter close around her but couldn't stop shivering. She knew her coldness came from the inside.

Exbury. How she hated that name. She'd changed her name legally to her mother's maiden name as soon as she possibly could, but every time she heard "Exbury," all she could remember was how her whole life had been shattered, her ivory tower destroyed. By lies. By deceit.

One minute she had been the naive, trusting young wife of a well-to-do young businessman. The next she was a widow without a cent to her name and suspected of being involved in his illegal activities.

The police had eventually dropped the investigation because of lack of evidence, but the reporters hadn't been willing to let things go. They'd kept after her until she'd lost her job. Until the friends she was staying with gently suggested that she find somewhere else to stay. Until she'd even begun to doubt herself. She started to question her faith in people and doubt her own judgment.

She'd been innocent of even knowledge of her husband's illegal fur-smuggling operation, but she'd always felt guilty. Guilty of ignorance, blindness, sheer stupidity.

Guilty, too, of lies of omission. Joey and Marge knew the truth about her, but Robin hadn't told anyone else. They all thought she was the innocent, independent, slightly skewed city girl who'd taken her small inheritance and tried to build a dream with it. She just never brought up the fact that she was also the widow of a man who'd been indicted for dealing in furs from endangered species.

If it came out that Robin McKenna was really Teresa Robin Exbury, she'd lose everything—including the grant funding. Money for protecting wildlife would never be given to the wife of a man who'd tried to profit from destroying it.

Dear Lord, it had already been five years—how long would it take to finally put the past behind her? Or would it always come back to haunt her? Burying her face in her hands, she finally released the silent, burning tears.

SIX

"Robin?"

Robin awakened to a gentle, husky voice calling her name and the warmth of a body next to her. "Hmm?"

"Feeling better?"

She felt the lightest of touches on her hair, but didn't open her eyes. The touch became a rhythmic stroking as he petted her the way he would a cat. She just smiled sleepily and snuggled farther under the warm comforter, wanting to sink back into the pleasant dream she'd been having. She couldn't remember much of it, but she knew Patrick had been in it too.

"Hey, sleepyhead." Patrick whispered the words close to her ear—so close she could feel his warm breath against her neck. When she felt his lips suck on her earlobe, her eyes flew open.

He chuckled warmly. "I thought that might get your attention. Are you feeling better?"

He was so close, their thighs touched, and it made Robin feel hemmed in. She sidled away, then yawned and wiped a hand across her eyes, still itchy from her recent tears. "What time is it? How long have I been asleep?"

"About an hour."

"Oh. The groceries . . ."

"I put them away."

"Thanks. I guess I'd better get up and feed the babies."

"I'd offer to help, but I'd better leave that to the expert. Is there something else I can do?"

Robin smiled a little. "No. It won't take long."

"But you do so much already, Robin. You didn't feel well earlier, so let me help you now, okay? Then you can come back inside and lie down again—I'll even make you a cup of hot tea. My mother always thought that was the cure for all ills."

She felt an unfamiliar warmth inside. He sounded genuinely worried about her, and it had been a long time since anyone had wanted to take care of her. Most of the people in town liked her a great deal but considered her the most capable woman they'd ever met. No one would have dreamed of trying to take care of her—not even Joey, and he was her best friend. She'd forgotten how nice it felt.

Instinctively she steeled herself. Hadn't she learned anything? How many of those crushing little reminders, like the radio news, did she need to learn to keep her distance? "I'm all right. And I just have to feed the little ones. It won't take long. Why don't you wait in here? I'll start on supper when I'm done. Do you like pasta? I think I have all the ingredients on hand."

Patrick nodded but didn't move, and his eyes never left her face.

"What are you looking at me like that for?"

"I like the way you look when you wake up. Your hair's tangled—"

"It's always tangled," she broke in.

He grinned. "Yeah. And your eyes are dark and sleepy-looking and—"

"And I have crease marks on my cheeks."

"I like crease marks." He ran a finger down the pink indentation on her face, then over the curve of her bottom lip. His maple-syrup gaze followed the path of his finger, then lingered warmly on her lips.

He was going to kiss her. Robin saw the message flash through his eyes and ducked away. "I'd better get moving," she said brightly, and unwrapped the comforter from around her. "I'll be back in about half an hour," she added, and bounded down the stairs.

Patrick's eyes narrowed in thought as he watched her go. Was she really all right or just pretending? He'd heard and recognized the name on the radio earlier just like she had. And he'd seen the shocked, hurt look in her eyes.

But why was it there? Was it there because she hated remembering what had to have been a painful, humiliating time or was it there because it hurt to remember a husband she'd loved in spite of what he'd done? He wondered if she still loved him.

Was that what he was fighting—the memory of a ghost? He wished he knew the truth. What had John Douglas Exbury done, and how had it affected Robin? He knew he could always call Bill Marsh again and find out, but he wanted Robin to tell him. That would mean she trusted him. And he needed her trust.

Still lost in thought, he made his way down the stairs and sat at the kitchen table. He blinked when he met the disgruntled gaze of the white cat who'd been dozing on a place mat in a ray of late-afternoon sun. Patrick just patted the feline absently and set it gently on the floor.

Whatever haunted Robin was enough to make

her feel ill. Patrick remembered the white, pinched look on her face, and his gut twisted. Nothing, nobody, should hurt her so much. He wanted to kiss the hurt away and make it better, but he didn't think she'd go for the idea. At least not yet. So he'd just do what he could. He stood decisively and began rummaging through the refrigerator, his every step watched by the always hungry cat keeping vigil next to the table.

As soon as Robin opened the door, she was greeted by the warm, delicious aromas of garlic, herbs, and tomatoes. Steam rose temptingly from a large pot on the stove. She looked at Patrick standing next to the stove with a dish towel tucked in the waistband of his jeans and a wooden spoon in his hand. His hair, more wavy than usual from the steam, looked endearingly rumpled.

She couldn't keep a mile from pulling at her lips. "What are you doing?"

Patrick turned and ran his free hand through his hair, adding to its dishevelment. "Hi. I'm your chef for the evening." He looked her over carefully.

Robin wondered if he could tell she'd been crying again. She'd tried to blot away the worst of the damage, but unlike some women, she didn't cry prettily. Her eyes puffed up, her nose turned red and dripped, her face blotched.

She saw him open his mouth to say something, then apparently change his mind. He turned back to the pot on the stove, dipped the spoon in, then held it under her nose. "Doesn't that smell heavenly?"

Robin inhaled deeply. "Wonderful. What is it?"

"Patrick Brady's authentic Italian spaghetti sauce."

"Authentic? C'mon. Brady's not exactly an Italian name."

"True. But D'Angelo is."

"Your mother's maiden name?"

"My mother's mother."

"This is so nice of you, Patrick. But you didn't need to go to all this trouble."

"Well, my grandma always said there were ordinary days, extraordinary days, and pasta days. And this seemed like it might be a pasta day for you." Patrick turned back to the stove and stirred the sauce again. "You want to talk about it?" he asked quietly.

Robin wouldn't meet his eyes as she said, "Talk about what? I just had a headache, that's all."

"Are you sure?"

"What do you mean? Of course, I'm sure!"

"Okay." Patrick accepted her answer easily enough. "Do you have any basil?"

"Basil?"

"You know, it's an herb that goes great in tomato sauces."

Robin made a face at him and rummaged through a kitchen drawer. "I know what basil is. So, do you need anything else?"

"You got any spaghetti noodles? The water's boiling."

"I'm not sure." She looked through the small closet that served as a pantry, then held up a box that had about a half-dozen pieces left in it. "I wouldn't think six noodles are enough."

Patrick frowned at the simmering sauce on the stove. "Well, I guess we could always eat it like soup."

"I bought a box of noodles at the grocery store this afternoon. Where did you put them?"

"What kind of noodles?"

"Rotini."

"What's rotini?"

"Your grandma's maiden name was D'Angelo and you don't know what rotini are?"

"You're an impudent child, aren't you?"

She stuck her tongue out at him. "Aha!" She snared the box of pasta and handed it to Patrick,

watching as he emptied it into the boiling water.
"Can I help?"

"You can sit down over here." He led her to
the kitchen table and pushed her gently into the
chair, then bent down to pick up the still watchful
white cat sitting next to the chair and put it in her
lap. "That cat keeps ogling me. Keep it busy."

"She keeps ogling you because she's a female.
I'd assume you're often ogled by females. You
should be used to it."

Maple-syrup brown eyes became gold as he
cast her a sidelong glance. "Are you saying you
like the way I look?"

"Me? No, I'm just saying *she* does." Robin
smiled a little.

Oh, he loved her smile. It crawled inside him
and lit a fire. He'd like to dedicate himself to
making sure she smiled often—at him. He made a
sweeping bow and flung out one hand dramati-
cally. "Now prepare to watch a master at work."

"Modest, aren't we?" Robin murmured.

"Honest." Patrick set the table with a flourish
and poured two glasses of tea. He set one in front
of her. "Not red wine, but a pleasing vintage,
nonetheless. Light, sweet, wonderful bouquet.
And the best of years."

"This year."

"Today. Taste it. This should be the best iced tea you've ever had."

Robin took a sip and smiled in pleasure. It was already sweetened and had just a touch of lemon. "Tell me about your Italian grandmother."

"Well, her parents actually came from Italy. The closest she's ever come is an Italian deli in Baltimore. She's not your typical grandmother, either. She hates to sew, and she makes cookies only once a year at Christmas. And then only under duress."

"What does she do?"

"She almost got my brothers and me arrested once."

"How'd she do that? How old were you?"

"Jason and I were in fourth or fifth grade and Sean was in second grade, I believe. We were staying with her for the weekend, and she took us with her to a sit-down demonstration in front of city hall. I can't even remember what it was about, but it turned into a real adventure. My parents weren't terribly amused at the time, though."

Robin giggled. "I think I like your grandmother already."

"And I think she'd like you."

"Was she into a lot of causes?"

"Still is. Everything from saving the whales to

protecting the penguins to banning toxic waste."

"How many grandchildren does she have all together?"

"Counting me? Twelve."

"How about your other grandmother?"

"She died when I was small. I don't remember much except that she had a long gray braid that she wore around her head and that she loved to read to us. So tell me about your grandparents."

"There's not much to tell. My mother's parents spent every summer in the south of France, so I only saw them at Christmas. They usually showed up with a beautiful and expensive doll." Robin shook her head. "Even when I was in my teens."

"How about your other grandparents?"

"They live in Oregon, but I usually spent a week there every summer with my parents. They're every child's fantasy. Grandma baked dozens and dozens of cookies and mailed a box to me every couple of weeks. She still does. Nearly every Christmas she'd make new dresses for my Barbie dolls, and Grandpa would always make a piece or two of furniture for my dollhouse."

"You sound like you love them a great deal."

"I do. I don't get to see them as much as I used to because I don't have enough money to fly out there, but I call them every week."

"What about your parents?"

"Daddy died ten years ago. Mom remarried six years ago and lives in Alaska."

"Alaska?"

Robin smiled. "Yeah. He's a college professor in Anchorage. It's hard to imagine my mother there, though. She used to complain whenever the temperature dropped below sixty."

Patrick checked the sauce on the stove and declared it *pèrfetto*. He turned and quickly dished up two plates of pasta.

"You're right," Robin said, after they'd eaten quietly for a few minutes. "You are a master. A master of pasta, anyway."

"Do you feel better?"

"Why do you keep harping on that?" she asked defensively. "I'm just fine."

"Anything you want to talk about? I'm willing to listen, Robin, if you've got a problem. And I care."

"Patrick, would you please just drop it?" Her voice was a little sharper than she intended and she added, "Thank you for caring, but nothing's wrong. I just felt a little under the weather. The pasta helped, though. It was very thoughtful of you."

"Thoughtful?" He grimaced. "Isn't that in the same category as sweet or nice?"

"Oh, I don't know. I certainly wouldn't dream of calling you either one of those." She took her empty plate to the sink.

Patrick walked over to her, placing his own plate in the sink. "You wash, I'll dry."

"We've got to put water on the stove to heat first," she said as she turned to do just that. "The pump only has cold water."

"Why don't you have plumbing put in here, anyway?"

"Too expensive. I could barely afford to do the bathroom. When I first moved in here, there was just a path."

"Path? What path?"

"To the outhouse."

"Outhouse?" Patrick asked incredulously. "You mean, no bathtub or—or anything? How'd you manage showers?"

"I didn't. I used to bathe in an old metal washtub. I had to heat the water on the stove."

Patrick had a sudden sharp image of Robin, her hair pulled up on top of her head, exposing the long line of her neck as she poured a kettle of hot water into a waiting tub. The steam would cause her hair to frizz into thousands of red-gold tendrils. Then she'd drop the towel to reveal . . . He called a sudden halt to his wayward thoughts as he felt a surge of warmth in his loins.

She was rapidly becoming an obsession with him. Maybe once he'd made love to her, he'd be able to get his mind on something else. Then again, maybe that would only make it worse.

Robin poured the hot water from the kettle into the sink, then added the dish-washing liquid. When she looked around for the sponge, she saw Patrick holding it.

"Can the dishes wait awhile?" he asked.

"I don't see why not." Robin shrugged. "Why do you ask?"

"I've got a sudden desire to try out that swing on your front porch. It's a gorgeous night."

Robin took the sponge out of his hand. "Go try it out, then. I'll finish the dishes."

Patrick took the sponge back and dropped it into the sudsy water. "It's positively un-American to sit in a porch swing alone. Didn't you know that?" He reached over and took her hand and tugged her outside. He sat, and pulled her down beside him. Close beside him.

Robin tried to inch over a little, but he wouldn't let her. He slipped his arm around her shoulders and snuggled her close to his side. She shifted her hips away, but he only pulled her shoulders even closer until she was leaning into him.

Patrick sighed contentedly. "The stars seem so close here, as if I could touch them. In D.C., there's always a haze around the horizon from all the lights. It's as if it never gets really dark. You know, when I was a child . . ."

How could he chatter on so casually? Robin wondered. Couldn't he hear her heart pounding? If he couldn't hear it, he had to feel it. After all, she was sandwiched between his arm and his side as closely as a hamburger between two halves of a bun.

The warmth of his body surrounded her, and she could smell his soapy, spicy fragrance—tinged with the lingering overtones of basil and oregano. It was a comforting, homey aroma. But the sensation of his hard body next to hers was anything but comforting. She was all tingling awareness and breathless anticipation.

Anticipation? What was she anticipating? She stole a glance at Patrick out of the corner of her eye. He still chatted on about something, but she couldn't follow it. It took all her powers of concentration just to keep her breathing steady.

The weight of his arm around her shoulders made her feel safe and secure. But the tips of his fingers as they traced little circles on her upper arm made her feel shaky and vulnerable. She was confused at the conflicting emotions.

"I need to go take care of the dishes." What had happened to her voice? It sounded so tremulous.

"You don't need to go anywhere," Patrick murmured in her ear.

"But—"

"Stay here. Talk to me."

"I don't know what to talk about."

"Tell me what you were like as a little girl. Were you a dainty little thing with ponytails and patent-leather shoes?"

It was hard to keep her thoughts focused on anything other than the feel of Patrick's arm around her, but she tried. "I, um, was more of a tomboy. Instead of ponytails and patent leather, I was more into pigtails and sneakers. I loved my dolls, though. For all of about an hour. Then I was ready to go outside and climb trees and ride bikes."

"I liked to climb trees too. I'd perch up out of reach of my brothers and read all afternoon."

"With your little dog in your jacket?"

"Sometimes. Drove the cat crazy trying to figure out where the barking was coming from."

They continued to talk long into the evening, Robin snuggled against his side. They shared memory after memory of childhood treats and pranks. Finally, Patrick leaned his head back a little so he could see her better. "I wish I'd known you as a little girl. We could've played baseball together."

"Ha! I'll have you know I was still in diapers when you were old enough to play baseball."

"I guess you were at that. Tomboy or not, though, you grew up to be an absolutely beautiful woman."

Robin stared at his eyes, fascinated by the warm glow of desire in them, then turned her head away. They didn't seem to bother Patrick, however, he simply took her earlobe between his teeth, running his tongue around the tiny gold stud she wore before reaching up to remove it. Robin snapped her head around in time to see him drop it into his shirt pocket.

His eyes met hers, and he smiled—slow, dark, and dangerous. She quivered when she saw it. Only Lucifer himself could have come up with a smile any sexier.

"It's a bit cool tonight. Don't you think?" she asked breathlessly.

"I'm warm."

"Oh. Um, I really ought to feed the owl. It's getting late. Do you want to come with me?"

"Later."

"Have you ever seen a barn owl close up?"

"No."

"They're beautiful. Their eyes are . . ." Patrick's lips traced a path down the side of her cheek. "Their eyes . . ." He placed a lingering kiss at the corner of her mouth. "Patrick . . ."

"Robin." It was all he said before his mouth covered hers. This kiss wasn't the tentative exploration of a man getting to know a woman, but a sure hungry possession. His lips knew just the way to move to make hers soften beneath them. His tongue knew just the way to dual to incite hers to fight back.

He turned toward her so the tips of her breasts touched his chest. Slowly he urged her closer, pressing her against him until he could feel her heart beating, pounding with the same erratic rhythm as his. His hands swept over the rough texture of her sweater, then slipped underneath to slide over the smooth, warm skin of her back.

Robin gasped softly and arched her body into his. As if that were the invitation he'd been waiting for, Patrick's hands moved around to englobe her breasts, their lace covering a sensual barrier to his seeking fingers. He unerringly found the hard tips, already straining against the fabric. When he stroked his thumbs over the beaded nipples,

Robin made a mewling sound deep in her throat and clutched his shoulders.

Seeking hands glided around to unfasten the clasp of her bra, then hungrily filled themselves with the warm weight of her small perfectly shaped breasts. With vague surprise, Patrick realized his hands were shaking. His desire for her ate away at him like acid, leaving him feeling hollow. Only her touch filled him up again.

He reluctantly removed his hands from her breasts, just long enough to pull at the buttons of his shirt. One, maybe two, popped off, but he didn't care. He tore open the front of his shirt, then lifted her sweater and pressed her into him.

The feeling of flesh against flesh was exquisite, and Patrick shuddered with pleasure. "Sweet, so sweet," he groaned against her lips. "God, you feel good next to me, Robin. Touch me, sweetheart. I'm dying for you to touch me." He kissed her again, searing hot and wet.

Robin hesitantly slid her hands from his shoulders down to his chest, accompanied by his hoarse encouragements. Her movements were slow and leisurely, as if she savored the lightly furred skin beneath her fingers. At her touch Patrick felt his heart thud, and he groaned again. Flames of desire surged through him. He wanted more. He needed more.

He lifted his lips from hers and drew her away from him, his eyes feasting on the creamy skin of her breasts. Their hardened tips appeared dark and shadowy in the reflected light from the door. He bent his head and closed his hungry lips over one ripe pouting tip, sucking and then licking it.

At Robin's indrawn breath, he turned his attention to the other one, teasing it, too, to aching awareness. Robin's hands clutched his hair, as if to hold him to her, and she arched her neck. Patrick nibbled a trail from one breast up the line of her throat to her kiss-reddened lips.

He pulled away only long enough to tug her sweater over her head and toss it aside. The movement caused the swing to sway gently, but the motion seemed just a part of the ebb and flow of the sensual tide that pummeled them. The scrap of pink lace she wore followed the sweater to the floor, and Patrick's hands moved lovingly over the soft curves finally displayed in their entirety to his eager gaze.

"Now it's your turn. Take off my shirt, sweetheart," Patrick urged, and Robin slid the material down his shoulders, then dropped it on top of the pile of clothing beginning to form next to the swing. She couldn't keep her hands from exploring every inch of his chest. It was broad and tan and dusted with crisp gold-brown curls. His shoulders were just the right size and shape to cradle a woman's head after making love.

She hardly noticed when Patrick popped open the snap on her jeans and loosened the zipper. But every nerve ending in her body came to instant tingling awareness when his hand slid down over her smooth, flat belly and tangled in the soft nest of curls at the apex of her thighs. Her heart skipped, her breath caught. She'd never felt this way before—never felt this liquid heat in her veins. Not even with John Douglas.

John Douglas. The name hit her like a slap in the face. "No." She wasn't even aware she was going to say it until the word popped out.

"What?" Patrick asked incredulously, as if he hadn't heard right.

"Patrick, no." Her voice sounded weak and thready, so she tried to put more force behind it. "We have to stop."

"What's the matter, sweetheart?"

"Nothing. This has gone far enough. I don't want this."

"You're wrong, sweetheart. It hasn't gone nearly far enough." When she tried to tug her hands away, he held them pressed flat against his chest. "Feel my heartbeat. It pounds that way because I want you so much. And you want me too. You know you do."

"We're not ready for this."

"Oh, we're ready, all right. Remember, I just touched you here"—he lightly brushed his fingers across the seam of her jeans—"and I found you hot and wet and ready for me. And I'm so ready, it hurts." He took her hand and pressed it to the hardness at the front of his jeans.

For a split second Robin's hand curled around his arousal, feeling its size and shape. Then she jerked her hand away and stood. She scooped up her sweater and turned her back to Patrick as she tugged it over her head. Hand on the screen door, she turned to say, "I won't deny my body may be ready, but my mind isn't."

"Then I'll just have to make love to your mind, won't I?"

The only answer to his question was the slamming of the screen door as Robin went inside. Patrick picked up the scrap of pink lace she'd left behind. Suddenly Robin reappeared and scooped her bra out of his grasp. The screen door slammed again. He sighed. She had a real talent for dramatic exits.

SEVEN

When Patrick woke up the next day, there was a note from Robin on the kitchen table and a plateful of sandwiches in the refrigerator. She was gone most of the afternoon, and when she did return, she made herself scarce, staying out in the enclosure or the garden.

It wasn't until supper that they finally had a chance to talk, and then the conversation was impersonal. Patrick could only admire Robin's skill in introducing discussions on music, politics, economic politics, foreign affairs, and books. She'd be a hit at the boring dinner parties he used to go to in D.C. He couldn't say he didn't thoroughly enjoy their spirited debates, but her apparent need to keep him at a distance bothered him.

As Robin did the dishes, silence reigned,

punctuated only by the clatter of plates and the clinking of glasses. When Patrick offered to help, she wordlessly handed him the dish towel. The silence was uncomfortable, but not cold. The air crackled with awareness.

Robin jumped every time Patrick so much as passed by her. Finally, he put his hands firmly on her upper arm and turned her to face him. "I'm not planning on throwing you over my shoulder and having my wicked way with you." He gave a lopsided grin. "However much I may want to."

"I know that," she snapped.

Patrick's eyes narrowed, and he cocked his head to one side. "Then stop acting like you expect it."

Robin bit her lip and stepped back. "I'm sorry. There's just something about you that makes me crazy."

"We're even, then. Because there's something about you that makes me want you like crazy." Yeah, he thought. Makes me want you on that bed over there or here on the floor or on the table, the counter, the porch swing. . . . He muffled an oath as he felt the unmistakable swelling in his lower body and grabbed his crutches to hobble out on the porch. Maybe he'd better call Joey and arrange to stay with him. God only knew that staying around Robin too much longer was going to wear out the front seam of his jeans.

But it wasn't just her body he wanted. Why hadn't he seen it before? He wanted her contagious smile, her restless energy, the gentle, tender compassion, the witty and wicked sense of humor. He wanted it all.

But he also wanted the truth. Her truth. He wanted to know the secrets that had made her cry yesterday, that were responsible for the shadows beneath her eyes today. Her secrets might not destroy Robin physically, the way Shelly's addiction had destroyed her, but he knew the secrets could wear Robin down emotionally.

"Patrick?" Robin's voice came from the screen door. "Is something wrong?"

Nothing that making love to you all night long wouldn't help. "Just needed some fresh air, that's all."

"I thought I'd fix a cup of coffee. I'll be glad to fix you one, if you don't mind instant."

"Thanks. Instant's fine."

"It'll be ready in a few minutes."

Patrick heard the phone ring. He couldn't quite hear her words, but Robin sounded delighted at the call. He hoped it wasn't Dudley Do-Right—he couldn't handle any more of him.

Casually—at least he tried to look casual—he sauntered back inside.

He immediately relaxed when he heard Robin say the word "Grandma" and leaned against the kitchen counter, watching the timer on the microwave count down. When the buzzer sounded, Patrick opened the door and took out the cup. He opened the jar of instant coffee and dipped in a spoon, ready to stir it into the cup of steaming water. There was no water in the cup. There was, however, a dead mouse.

With a loud clatter, the spoon dropped onto the kitchen counter, scattering coffee crystals everywhere. Patrick heard a muffled giggle from Robin, who'd apparently seen the whole thing. She murmured her good-byes, then hung up the phone. With an amused grin, she surveyed Patrick's baffled expression.

"Is this the latest way to drink coffee?" he asked wryly. "If so, I'm not sure it'll catch on. Unless you're a cat, that is. You knew I was going to do this, didn't you?"

Robin looked at him with wide, innocent eyes. "How could I possibly know that you were going to come in here and rummage through the microwave? Besides, this is the way I always defrost mice."

"Why do you have to defrost them? What on earth do you do with them?"

"This is the owl's supper." Robin went to the refrigerator and opened the top freezer. She pulled out a plastic bag containing perhaps a dozen frozen rodents, then stuffed them back in with a grimace. "It's not my favorite thing, but owls and other raptors, like hawks and eagles, are carnivorous. Dog food just doesn't cut it."

"Uh, where do you get the mice?"

"Joey provides them. I don't even ask where *he* gets them. I don't want to know."

Patrick peered down into the coffee cup again. "It's not much bigger than the baby squirrels you have out there now."

"I know. As I said, I don't like it, but raptors have to eat too. I keep telling myself the mice are just food. I know it's a cop-out, but . . ." She shrugged and picked up the cup. "Let me run feed the owl, then I'll come back and fix the coffee, unless you want to. You know how to use a microwave, don't you?"

"Sure, but I'd like to watch you feed the owl, since you didn't tell me when you went out to do it last night."

"There's not much to see, really. Sometimes he eats right away; other times he just stares at me until I leave. And when he does eat, it's not very pretty."

"I don't mind. I'm interested in everything you do."

Robin searched his face, not sure what she expected to see. Maybe amusement or mild curiosity. Instead, she saw something indefinable, but warm and earnest and real.

Patrick followed her out to the shelter and watched as she donned her leather gloves and laid the mouse in the bottom of the cage. The owl blinked one eye, then the other, and stared at her, but otherwise made no move.

"I guess it's going to be one of those nights," she murmured, and turned to check on the other cages.

She stopped in her tracks and watched as Patrick checked the temperature controls on all the heating pads to make sure they were on. He then opened the door to the possum's cage and added fresh water from the jug she always kept ready. When he reached in one of the cages to rearrange the terry cloth "blanket" over the nest of baby squirrels, she found a tender smile stealing over her lips.

"You know, for all your talk about bees in my bonnet and bats in my belfry, you don't seem to mind the animals all that much."

Patrick shrugged and mumbled, "They're all right."

He seemed embarrassed at having been found out. Maybe he thought that soft spot didn't belong in a macho male. Whether it belonged there or not, Robin was totally charmed by it.

She continued to watch Patrick until he looked up. "What are you looking at me like that for?"

"I'm trying to figure you out."

"Hey, I'm not complicated."

"Yes, you are," she murmured. "More than I thought." He was a reporter, true, but he was also a warm, witty, compassionate, and utterly sexy man. She got a strange feeling inside every time she looked at him—a feeling she was afraid to examine too closely.

Patrick took a step closer and reached out a hand, running it down the side of her face. "I'm just a man, Red. A man who wants you very much."

"Patrick . . ."

"I know. You're not ready yet. I'll wait till you are. As long as it takes." He stepped closer, slipping one hand behind her head, and brought up his other hand to catch a tendril of hair, rubbing it between his fingers. "It's so silky." His voice lowered to a guttural whisper. "I've dreamed about your hair. Of spreading it over my pillow. Of tangling my fingers in it as we make love. Have you ever thought about making love with me, Robin? Our bodies feel so good next to each other, and our lips seem to fit together perfectly. . . ."

Robin was bewitched into silence by his hot, wicked, seductive words. He told her all the things he wanted to do to her, with her. He promised her they'd touch the stars together.

"Patrick?" Her thready voice was a plea. But she didn't know whether she wanted him to stop or to continue weaving his sensual word spell. The decision was taken out of her hands by the blare of a car horn that split the silence. Their eyes still clung for one breathless moment, then both turned and went out to see what all the racket was.

It was Don Yoncey and his twelve-year-old son, Marcus. They lived about a half mile down the road. As soon as they saw Robin, Don called out to her, "We got an injured deer in the back of the truck." Robin ran to the bed of the truck and waited for Marcus to let down the gate before crawling up next to the unconscious animal.

"Looks like a yearling," volunteered the boy, and Robin nodded. Marcus helped her out on occasion after school or on weekends.

"Don, you want to pull your truck on around back to the barn? I'll have to put her in there. Did you call the animal clinic?"

Shaking his head, Don fished his keys out of his back pocket. "Just found her on Old West Road. We was comin' home from prayer meetin'." He climbed back in the cab and started up the engine.

Patrick climbed up on the truck bed beside Robin. "What can I do to help?"

"They'll carry her into the barn. There should be a bed of straw they can lay her on."

"I can help Don carry her."

Robin simply indicated his wrapped ankle. "How about if you hobble in the house and call the clinic? The number's by the phone."

Don and Marcus carried the doe into the barn. She wasn't heavy, but with the two of them, it was easier to carry her without perhaps causing more damage than had already been done.

"We found her by the side of the road. Reckon she was hit by a car?" asked Don.

"Probably." Robin looked up from the injured animal to Patrick, who'd just reentered the barn. "Did you get hold of anybody at the clinic?"

"I got hold of the receptionist. She said the other vet is in Roanoke for her son's emergency appendectomy, and she isn't sure where Joey is. He's not at the clinic or at home. I left a message for him to come here as soon as he can."

"Good," Robin murmured absently, her hands running gently over the deer. Already, though, her experience was telling her it didn't look good. There seemed to be several broken ribs, and heaven only knew what kind of internal injuries. She got to her feet. "I've got to get some supplies. Patrick, stay with her, and if she comes around, don't let her try to get up."

Don and Marcus followed Robin outside and stopped next to the truck. "Think you can do anything for her, Miss McKenna?" the young teenager asked.

"I don't know, Marcus, but I'll try. I promise."

She absently watched the headlights of their truck cut through the deepening twilight as she hurried to the beat-up old cabinet she kept in the enclosure. She pulled open the top drawer and rummaged through the supplies until she'd snagged a bottle of antibiotic pills. Maybe they would help, maybe they wouldn't; she just felt as if she had to do something until she got hold of Joey.

When she reentered the barn, Patrick was stroking the doe's head and talking to it quietly.

The animal had regained consciousness and looked up at him with liquid brown eyes curiously free of fear. Robin quickly pulverized a couple of tablets, mixed them with water, and filled a syringe with the liquid. She pulled back the corner of the animal's mouth and squirted in the antibiotic.

Robin watched Patrick a moment as he continued to talk soothingly to the young deer. He looked up and met her gaze. "She's so beautiful. I'd never realized how soft they were. Do you think she'll be all right?"

Robin shrugged. "I don't know, Patrick. I wish Joey would get here. In the meantime, all I can do is clean the abrasions on her legs and hope the antibiotics help."

"Is there anything else I can do?"

"No, just keep her quiet and still." She grabbed a folded blanket and flicked it open, laying it over the animal. Her movements were capable and professional, but Patrick thought she seemed cool, unruffled, even distant.

She left and came back a few minutes later with cotton balls and hydrogen peroxide. When Robin dabbed at the abrasions on the front leg, the doe jumped a little. Again Patrick gentled it. The cuts and scrapes on the hind legs must not hurt much, because he noticed the doe didn't flinch at all when Robin cleaned them.

When she finished, Patrick pulled the blanket back over the doe's legs and continued to stroke the soft fur on its neck and head until he was sure it closed its eyes. He then turned to Robin, who was sitting on a bale of straw in the corner. "Well, what do we do now?"

"Wait for Joey to come by. I think I'll bring out a blanket and stay right over there."

"She seems okay, don't you think?"

"I really don't know. There don't seem to be many external injuries, but I know there are some broken ribs. I'm not sure about internal injuries." She hesitated a moment, then added, "Don't get your hopes up too high."

"Don't be such a pessimist, Red. She'll be fine." Patrick went in to place another call to Joey, while Robin gathered some blankets. When he returned to the barn, she'd already spread the blankets out on a bed of straw. She sat, her arms hugging her knees, and stared pensively at the sleeping doe.

"You look worried." Patrick sat next to her and leaned back against the rough plank wall.

"I am."

"Well, don't be. She's quiet, and by morning

she'll be okay. She probably just got shook up a little."

Robin wanted to tell him she had a bad feeling about this, that the reason the doe rested so quietly was probably because her hind legs were paralyzed. She didn't say either of those things. She couldn't.

Patrick was looking at the deer with all the awed fascination of a child who'd just peeked under the Christmas tree. Besides, maybe, just maybe, she was wrong, and everything *would* be all right in the morning. She sighed, not believing it for a minute.

They sat in companionable silence, listening to the radio Robin had brought in. Patrick draped his arm about her shoulders and tugged her a little closer. It made her think of the porch swing, and her body came alive with remembered desire. Now, however, instead of feeling hot and over-whelmed with sheer masculine menace, she felt warm and comforted by his strength.

They talked quietly for hours, though Robin kept a close eye on the deer. Privately, it disturbed her that the animal hadn't even tried to get up. But at least she was resting comfortably and wasn't in any pain. She continued to withhold her worries from Patrick. He didn't seem to want to hear it. Every time she even mentioned it, he shrugged off her comments.

Patrick had really taken to the deer, she thought as she stifled one of many yawns. It was a few minutes past midnight—and several hours past her usual bedtime. Patrick seemed wide awake as he finished reading chapter eleven of *Small Mammal Care*. He stopped reading now and then to ask Robin the occasional question. He was still reading when Robin fell asleep, her head cradled on his shoulder.

She awoke to the warmth of a hard male body nestled next to her. For one brief, heart-stopping moment, she thought the dream she'd been having was real—that she and Patrick *had* made love and fallen asleep in each other's arms. When she shifted position and became aware of the roughness of the old army blanket beneath her cheek, she remembered where she was. Battling a strange disappointment, she eased away from the embrace that held her close to his body.

He still slept soundly and would for some time, Robin realized when she picked up the book he'd been reading. From the location of the bookmark, he'd obviously read for several hours after she'd dozed off last night. She resisted the temptation to sit and watch him sleep. Instead, she went over to check on the deer.

The doe was alive and comfortable and less in shock than the night before, but still making no move to get to its feet. She offered it a few sips of water, then went to check on the animals out in the shelter.

After she had finished feeding the animals and cleaning the cages, Robin took a shower and fastened her hair back in a serviceable braid. She couldn't resist peeking in on Patrick every so often, but he slept on. He was every bit as much a night owl as she was a morning lark, she realized. Just one more difference between them.

Finally, about one o'clock, she brought a tray out to the barn and set it on the floor next to the blanket. Patrick lay on his back, one arm flung over his head, his dark wavy hair tousled over his forehead. His long eyelashes lay like ebony smudges on his cheeks. Robin reached out a hand to smooth the hair off his face.

"Patrick?" He didn't budge. She tapped his shoulder. "Patrick." She smiled when he mumbled groggily, then brushed her fingertips across his lips, down the side of his throat to the neck of his sweatshirt. Her fingers sneaked just inside. Patrick mumbled again. "Patrick," she purred, and ran a hand over his chest. "Wake up, Sleeping Beauty."

Patrick's fingers snapped closed around Robin's wrist, holding her hand against his chest. "Wrong. You're doing it all wrong." His eyes opened and surveyed her—sleepy, hazy with appreciation.

"Doing what wrong?"

"Here, let me show you." Patrick sat up and gently pushed Robin onto her back. He cupped her face between his hands and ran his thumbs over her eyelids, closing them. "Sleeping Beauty was awakened with a kiss."

Robin's eyes flew open, but Patrick again stroked his thumbs across her eyelids. "Now I'm going to do my best Prince Charming impression," he said, and kissed her. He tantalized, he coaxed, he teased, until Robin fastened an impatient hand at the back of his neck and held his head down to hers.

That was all the invitation he needed, and he advanced. Like a storm trooper, he invaded, blitzing her defenses. His greedy tongue swirled through her mouth again and again, while his plundering hands swirled around her breasts. He pushed her sweater and bra out of the way and buried his face between her breasts, then drew one nipple between his lips and stroked it to hardness with his tongue.

Robin clutched his hair. "Um, Prince Charming?" She felt light-headed and drew in a deep breath. It didn't help. *He* was the source of her dizziness. Cupping her breasts, he circled her nipples with his thumbs. "Patrick? I . . ."

He groaned. "I know, I know. You're not ready." He immediately tugged her sweater down and gently pulled her to a sitting position.

Robin wasn't sure just what she'd been about to say, but she hadn't planned on stopping him. It was just as well that he'd assumed she was going to, though, she realized when she heard a car engine. She hastily straightened her clothes and headed outside.

It was the truck from the wildlife center. Even though she was disappointed not to see Joey, she masked it and smiled. "Hi, Mike. Hi, Bernie."

"How goes it, Robin?" A tall, thin young man hopped out of the cab of the truck.

"I've got a badly injured deer in the barn and can't get hold of the vet. Other than that, everything's fine."

"Sorry about that. Is there anything I can do?"

"Not unless you're a vet, I'm afraid."

Bernie grimaced. "That bad?"

Robin saw Patrick standing in the barn doorway. She gave a short nod. "Let's get these animals for you. You can take the cages too. Just bring them back next time you pass this way, okay?" She walked to the enclosure, followed by the two men.

The fox, rudely awakened from her morning nap, growled a little and yipped. "She's about ready to be released," Robin remarked. "She just needs a couple of days moving around on that leg to limber it up."

Patrick limped out to the shelter, and Mike and Bernie eyed him curiously as they carried the cage out to the back of the covered truck and secured it. They smiled and nodded and murmured their howdies as they lifted the cage with the smaller of the two deer into the back.

"I didn't know you'd hired on help since we were here last," said Mike, a slightly plump middle-aged man. "If I'd known you were looking for somebody, I'd have sent over my son."

Robin smiled weakly. "This was sort of a spur-of-the-moment decision."

"And I just happened to be here," volunteered Patrick.

When the second deer had been secured in the back of the truck, Mike and Bernie closed the doors. "Any others ready to go?"

"Not yet, guys. I have a few woodchucks I'll be releasing in another few days. And I'll have an owl ready to go this weekend, but I'll be releasing her here. Do you have anything else for me?"

"Got a litter of squirrels in the front of the truck," answered Bernie, as he opened the door and maneuvered out the wire cage. "It's seven of them, from two litters, actually, about a week apart. And Mike'll be up here in a couple of days with another fox off the critical list and an eagle recuperating from a shooting last weekend. And, of course, we'll be able to rustle up the odd possum or two."

Robin took the cage of squirrels and handed it to Patrick. "Can you take that in for me?"

Patrick took the cage and slowly headed toward the shelter just as Bernie came over to Robin. "You want to go to the Friday night dance at the Catholic church? We had such a good time last month. I could pick you up about seven."

Patrick set the cage down and walked purposefully back over to Robin. He gave a patently false smile. "Sorry, she already has a date."

Bernie looked down at Patrick's bandaged ankle. "With you?"

"With me." Patrick picked up the cage and stalked off into the shelter.

Robin sighed. "I guess I do, at that," she muttered.

"I didn't know you were seeing anybody."

Patrick came back outside. "It's a recent development."

With a pained expression on her face, Robin agreed dryly. "Real recent."

"I guess I'll see you in a couple of days, then." Bernie climbed into the truck.

Robin waved, then turned to Patrick. "What the hell do you think you're doing? First with Earl, now this. You're acting like—like you own me."

"No, I'm just warning the other predators off my territory."

"I'm not your territory!"

Patrick took a step toward her. "Shall I prove otherwise?"

Robin held up her hands. "Don't you touch me, Patrick Brady! That doesn't prove anything."

"It proves how much we want each other. It proves how right we are together."

"It proves nothing but a little basic elementary male/female attraction. That's all."

"It proves a hell of a lot more than that! By the way," he said to Robin's retreating back, "pulling your hair back like that is criminal."

She may have walked off in the middle of this skirmish, but overall Patrick wasn't unhappy with the way things were going. She hadn't necessarily been gracious about it, but she had gone along with his statement that he was her date for the Friday night dance. Sprained ankle notwithstanding.

And the most important thing of all—regardless of what she said or how much she protested—in his arms, she melted like butter in the sun.

"Hey, Robin. Were you looking for me?" Joey poked his head in the shelter where Robin had just fed the owl and was tucking in all the baby animals for the night.

She immediately stopped what she was doing. "Where on God's green earth have you been?"

"I drove to Hampton to pick up Marge and Betsy. I had the day off, so I decided to stay overnight. So what's the problem? Did you call Susan?"

"I called Susan, but her son had emergency surgery over in Roanoke yesterday, so she closed the clinic for twenty-four hours. Anyway, Don Yoncey brought an injured doe here last night."

"How is she?"

"You need to take a look at her—but it doesn't look good. She doesn't respond at all from the middle of her back down."

They headed out to the barn. "Where's Trick?"

"Well, he's taken quite a liking to that deer, and he's sitting with her. Funny, too, but she does seem to stay calmer when he talks to her. I think she likes his voice."

"I guess you've discovered one of Trick's well-kept secrets."

"What, that he likes deer?"

"That he has a soft spot the size of Lake Michigan."

"He hides it well, but I've caught a glimpse or two. And it's that soft spot that worries me. He's not going to want to have the doe put down."

"You'll hate it every bit as much as he does, if not worse."

"You think I'd be used to it by now," she said ruefully.

Joey shook his head. "I'm not used to it by now. I do it because sometimes it's necessary."

"I know." The two friends shared a smile, then opened the door to the barn. Patrick sat on the straw next to the deer, talking softly and stroking its head.

"Hey, Joey. Glad you got here. She seems more alert today."

Robin watched as Joey bent down and ran his skilled hands over the deer, talking to it all the while. He looked up and caught her eye. She nodded. "Do what you have to do. Patrick, you want to come outside for a minute?"

Patrick followed her out. "What's going on?"

Robin stared out over the little meadow, watching as twilight shadows slowly filled it. She took a deep breath and forced the words out. "He's got to put her down."

He stared at her blankly. "What do you mean, 'put her down'?"

She continued to look away from Patrick. "He's got to put her to sleep."

"You mean kill her? No. No! She's better this morning, Robin. Stop him." He took a step toward the door, but Robin grabbed his arm with both hands.

"It's necessary, Patrick. Leave him alone."

"*Necessary?*" Patrick shouted. "What do you mean, necessary? You just don't want to mess with her. What, is it too much trouble for you?"

Robin stared at him in stony silence. Joey came out of the barn and looked from Robin to Patrick and back. "It's done."

She nodded brusquely. "Can you dispose of her?"

Patrick's voice was cold. "Like so much trash. Isn't that right, Robin?"

Robin flinched from the bitter sarcasm in his voice and turned and followed Joey back into the barn.

"He's not taking it well," Joey remarked unnecessarily. He hoisted the animal in his arms, carried it out to his car, opened the trunk, and set the animal down, then turned to Patrick.

"You've always been quick on the trigger, and most of the time you're right on the money. But this time, Trick old son, you're way off target. And I think you know it too. You made a huge mistake."

Patrick paced up and down. "What mistake? She just decided it was going to be too much trouble, so—"

"Do you really think that a woman who keeps three-legged raccoons, one-winged ducks, and descented skunks around is going to decide that one deer is too much trouble? The doe was paralyzed."

"Paralyzed?" Patrick stopped dead.

"There's something else you need to know. Robin has never made this decision lightly. It causes her a great deal of pain. But she realizes that sometimes it's the only humane thing to do."

Patrick ran a hand through his hair. "I really blew it, didn't I? God, Joey, I'm sorry."

"You're telling it to the wrong person, buddy."

"Yeah." He started to go toward the barn, then turned back. "How is she at forgiveness, anyway?"

"I'm not sure, but she could teach porcupines how to be prickly."

Patrick sighed. "Don't I know it!"

"Let me ask you something. How do you feel about her?"

"She's the most exasperating, stubborn, annoying . . ." Patrick took a deep breath and let it out slowly. "God help me, Joey. I think I'm in love with her."

Joey didn't look at all surprised. "So what happened to 'Travel often, travel light'?"

"Damned if I know!"

EIGHT

Patrick watched Joey drive away while he tried to think of what to say to Robin. He owed her a major apology. The things he'd said had been inexcusable, and she had every right to throw his words—or whatever else she had at hand—right back in his face. He hoped she wouldn't.

Patrick called himself every name he could think of and made up a few besides. How could he have accused her of being heartless? He knew that despite her tough armor, inside she was all gooey marshmallow.

When he opened the door, he saw Robin, her back to him, raking the straw. "Robin?"

She didn't answer. Patrick could hear the dull thud of the rake as she continued to groom the straw with measured strokes. Well, if the mountain wouldn't go to Muhammad . . .

He walked around and stood in front of her. Her eyes sparkled with tears, and more tears left silvery trails down her cheeks. Once in a while she gave a dainty sniff through her pink nose. Patrick felt a sudden tightness in his chest. She looked so delicate and fragile and hurt.

Then he met her gaze. If eyes had teeth, she'd have chewed him up and spit him out. "Robin," he began hesitantly. "God, I'm so sorry, honey."

"Is that the kind of person you think I am?" She bit the words out between clenched teeth.

"Of course not."

"You stay in my house, more trouble than a dozen injured dear, sit at my table, eat my food. I did your damned laundry, for Pete's sake. And you can accuse me of finding one poor injured doe too much trouble?"

Patrick winced. "I know. I'm sorry. I was wrong. I know that. I knew it all along."

"There's nothing you can say to make it any better," Robin said huffily. "Go back inside and pack your suitcase. I don't want you here."

"For God's sake, Robin. I'm as sorry as I can be. What else do you want me to say?"

Her eyes were bleak as she said, "I want you to say good-bye."

"You can't mean that."

"Can't I? I've decided that you're too much

trouble, Mr. Brady, so I'll simply dispose of you like an injured deer."

"I made a mistake, dammit. I admit it. I'll shout it from the top of your house, if you want. But you can't just get rid of me like yesterday's garbage."

"Do I pack your suitcase for you?"

"I'm not going anywhere, Red. And I'm not going to let you throw away what's good between us."

"There is no 'us'!" Robin denied.

"The hell there isn't! I'll prove it to you." Patrick stepped closer, his eyes gleaming with determination.

Robin held the rake up with both hands, as if it would form a barrier between them.

Patrick wrenched it out of her hands and tossed it aside, then grasped her wrists. She struggled against his iron grip.

"Let me go, damn you!"

"I've got some things to prove to you first." Patrick's voice was steel hard beneath its silkiness. "And the first thing I need to prove to you is that there *is* an 'us.' Then I need to prove to you how good 'us' can be." He jerked her to him.

"Let me go," Robin said, her voice weaker this time.

"Not for a long time, Red."

Robin tried to pull her wrists away, but his grasp was unrelenting. She opened her mouth to again demand he let her go, and Patrick took advantage of the moment to cover her lips with his.

He ground his mouth over hers in a kiss that contained as much possession as persuasion. His tongue swept over hers in a series of seductive silken thrusts. When he relinquished his hold, her hands went to his chest to push him away, but stayed there.

Patrick lifted his mouth from hers only long enough to grab the hem of her sweater and tug it over her head. Before Robin could protest, he caught her mouth in another deep, sweet, drugging kiss. When he looked down and saw the delicate lavender lace of her bra, he shook his head. "Lingerie designed to drive a man crazy," he murmured shakily and unfastened her bra, sliding it down her arms.

Robin choked out, "Patrick . . ." but whatever else she'd planned to say was lost as his hands filled themselves with her breasts. He rolled her nipples between thumbs and forefingers, and she moaned against his mouth.

She didn't even realize she'd unbuttoned Patrick's shirt until her fingers tangled in the soft curls of hair on his chest. She wasn't ready for this, she told herself, but her heart screamed, "Liar!" Maybe her mind wasn't ready, but her body was. Her breasts were swollen and aching for his caress, her nipples beaded tightly and screaming for his lips. And that secret place between her thighs was moist in readiness for his possession.

She wasn't afraid of sex. John Douglas hadn't been a cruel man, just a selfish one. But somehow she knew there had to be more to lovemaking than what she'd found with him, and she knew Patrick would be the one to show her just how much more. For the first time in years she listened to her heart, not her head, as she smoothed her hands across his chest, pushing his shirt aside.

"That's it," Patrick's voice rumbled deep in his chest. "Touch me, honey, touch me." She tilted her head, intent on watching what her hands did. She turned the tables on him, though, when her fingernails scratched gently at his flat brown male nipples. Patrick groaned.

When her hands moved to the buckle of his belt, he managed to pick her up and walked the few steps to the army blanket before his shaky knees and ankle gave out altogether. He set her back on her feet next to the blanket, his head swimming with her nearness. He'd wanted her so much, for so long, he couldn't believe it was happening now.

He only hoped his control held up long enough to bring her pleasure, but every touch of her hands pushed him closer and closer to the edge. He lost a little control when her hands slid the belt from his trousers. He lost a little more when she popped the metal snap at his waist, and lost more still when she teasingly ran her fingernail down his zipper.

"Slow down, Red Robin. We've got all night," he whispered, then grasped her hands in his and brought them up to his lips, where he pressed a kiss on the back of her fingers. "It's my turn to touch you now. Do you remember all those things I told you I wanted to do?"

Robin nodded, and her lashes fluttered, then closed, as Patrick's hoarse whisper surrounded her. He suited his actions to his words and described what he was doing to her as he did it. His words were silenced only when he gently drew her down on the blanket and began to explore her body with his hands and lips.

Why, oh why, had she thought she wasn't ready for this? She'd been ready for this all her life. Her lips, her breasts, the hollow of her neck, all received thorough and loving attention until Robin quivered with need. Only then did he slide her jeans down and cup her feminine warmth through the lavender satin panties she wore.

"Patrick?" she pleaded, not to stop him but to urge him on to quench the thirst she had—an unbearable, burning, needing thirst.

"Not yet, honey," he murmured as he slipped her panties off, then began to explore her womanly secrets. Had he ever seen another woman made as perfectly as she? How could it be that her breasts were just the right size for his hand, her nipples just the right shape and texture for his lips? Would she fit him as perfectly elsewhere? His fingers probed. She would. She'd fit him so perfectly that he'd probably go insane with it.

She gasped and moved against his seeking fingers. He stroked her again, intimately, eliciting another gasp and a plea. "Patrick?"

He paused for a moment and looked at her, needing to reassure himself that she was here, ready for him. God, she was beautiful—and never more so than now. Her lips were red and swollen from his kisses, her features tight with need. The rose-pink tips of her petal-soft breasts were achingly, temptingly hard. Her eyes—Patrick swallowed hard—her eyes were wide and unfocused and gold. A man could fall into those eyes and never come out again. At least not with his heart intact.

He ran his hand down her body from breasts to hip, and her eyes widened further, the gold blazing. Her hands, those restless hands, curled around his back and pulled him closer to her as she offered her lips to his. He kissed her again, groaning when her still-questing hands smoothed down his back to the denim stretched tight across his lean buttocks.

Gentle, teasing fingers slipped just beneath the waistband, but that was all the invitation Patrick needed. He rolled onto his back and shucked his jeans and underwear quickly, tossing the heavy denim across the straw-covered floor. Then he turned back to her and drew her into his arms. They both caught their breath when their bodies touched.

"Tell me what you're going to do to me now," Robin purred, her body moving sinuously against his.

"Now?" Patrick murmured against the side of her neck. "I can't remember my own name right now, Red. I'm so on fire for you, I'll burst into flames if I wait any longer."

In answer to his unspoken plea she parted her legs so he moved full against her body. "I'm burning up, too, Patrick," she whispered, her face flushed with desire. "I want it all now."

He levered himself up on his arms, his body

ready to possess hers. "Are you protected, Robin?"

Robin stared at him blankly. "Protected?"

"Birth control, honey."

"Oh. Um, no."

His body all but screamed in anguish when he rolled over on his back and stared up at the ceiling.

"Don't you have anything?" Robin's voice was husky with longing.

Taking a deep breath, he sat up and ran both hands through his hair, praying for the hot, pulsing need to simmer down a little so he could think. "No. Not even the obligatory one in my wallet." He smiled grimly.

He heard the straw beneath the blanket rustle as she sat up behind him, wrapping her arms around him. Patrick nearly groaned aloud when he felt the softness of her breasts press into his back.

"The timing is probably all right," she murmured against his skin.

He gritted his teeth against the need that shot through him. "Are you sure?"

"No." Her soft breath blew gently across his back as she sighed.

"Then we wait."

"Suppose I'm willing to take the risk?"

"Honey, I'm not willing to let you take the risk."

"So what do we do now?"

"I don't suppose you have a burning need to run by the drugstore for some"—he turned to her and brushed a kiss across her lips—"toothpaste?"

Robin smiled and returned the kiss. "Or maybe some . . . shampoo?"

Patrick smiled back and kissed her again. "Or some . . . aspirin, cold tablets, face cream?"

Robin wrapped her arms around him, torturing herself with the feeling of her soft breasts pressed against his hard, lightly furred chest. "Ah, I think I'm out of all those things. I definitely need to go into town for them."

He rubbed his chest against hers. "All of them?"

"Mmm. And if I'm not out of them, I'm sure I can think of something I'm out of."

"Is the drugstore going to be open? It's probably close to eight."

"We don't exactly roll up the sidewalks around here until nine. It'll still be open."

"I guess we'd better get dressed then," Patrick said reluctantly.

"We certainly don't want to shock the little old gray-haired druggist."

"Hey, I might give her a thrill."

"Him."

"Oh. Button up, honey."

The drive into town was so electric that Robin was vaguely surprised they didn't set off sparks whenever they touched. Since his ankle didn't seem to be bothering him much, Patrick drove, and Robin enjoyed watching him. Her eyes followed the lines of his face again and again—the sharply defined features, determined jawline, surprisingly sensual lips.

She just now realized she loved him, and her heart savored the words. She couldn't say the idea hit her like a ton of bricks; instead knowledge of it seeped into her slowly, filling her up inside. It was something she knew just as she knew the sun would rise in the morning, the leaves would change in autumn, and the columbines would bloom in spring.

Love didn't frighten her the way she'd always thought it would. Instead, she felt warm and safe and secure. She didn't know if he loved her back and, right now, didn't care. She knew she'd care later, but now her love was so new and so encompassing that she only needed for him to take what she offered.

She did notice that he looked at her differently

than he had before—his eyes warm and dark and tender. Maybe it was the way a man always looked at a woman he desired and was about to go to bed with, but Robin never remembered John Douglas looking at her like this. She felt beautiful and desirable when Patrick looked at her. All she'd ever felt when her husband looked at her was inadequate.

Funny, for the first time in years, the thought of her former husband didn't leave Robin with that panicky tightening in her chest. Less than forty-eight hours ago, the memories had been enough to make her ill; now she felt only a moment's regret for the foolish, blind innocent she'd been.

Robin showed Patrick where to park, and hand in hand they walked into the drugstore. The small store had a wonderfully old-fashioned flavor to it. There was a glass case up front full of "penny candy," and a counter along one wall where sodas and ice-cream floats were still served. Of course, Patrick also noticed some concessions to the changing times in the rack of videos for rent and the display of microwave popcorn next to the cash register.

When the pharmacist greeted Robin with a warm smile and invited her to sample a new candy bar he was carrying, Patrick frowned. "I thought you said he was little, old, and gray-haired," he muttered when the pharmacist turned to greet another customer.

Robin grinned. "Well, he *is* gray-haired."

"But he's not little or old," retorted Patrick, still watching the six-feet-tall prematurely gray man.

"He's very married, in case you're interested."

"How married?"

"His wife works here too. You know, you seem to have a problem with anyone of the male persuasion even talking to me."

"I don't know what you mean."

"Earl, Bernie, and the grocer?"

With an effort Patrick managed to keep from squirming. "They all leer at you."

"Leer?" Robin looked at him innocently and clasped his arm with hers, managing to rub her breasts across it in the process.

"Yeah, like this." Patrick rolled his eyes at her, then fastened his gaze directly on her chest.

Even though he was only joking, Robin could still feel her nipples tighten in response. "Gee, you are a world-class leerer."

"Is that really a word?"

"Maybe not, but it says what I want it to, so what does it matter?"

"I'm world-class in other things too," Patrick murmured suggestively.

"Well then," she purred, "we'd better get what we came in here for and go home so you can put your money where your mouth is."

"I can think of several places I'd like to put my mouth, but on money isn't one of them. So where are they?"

Robin turned down another aisle, and Patrick stopped dead at the huge display of various birth-control methods—including the largest selection of male protection he'd ever seen. "Ohmigod," he said in awe. "Not only a rainbow of colors, but stripes and polka dots too. Incredible. Why such a huge selection?"

Robin shrugged. "I don't know. Maybe it's because there's nothing else to do at night when everything closes up at nine o'clock. It's certainly an impressive display, isn't it?"

"Do you have a preference?"

"Anything."

Patrick made his selection, and they walked toward the front of the store. Suddenly, Robin stopped dead in her tracks. "Patrick, I can't go up there. He knows me, and when he sees those, he'll know we—I—we . . ."

"So?" Patrick pulled her into his arms and

kissed her, a brief but thoroughly possessive kiss that left her breathless. "Do you care?"

Dazed, Robin shook her head. "No, I guess I don't."

He grabbed a couple of boxes of microwave popcorn and a jar of vitamins and set them on the counter too. "Maybe he won't notice them mixed in with this stuff," he whispered to Robin and she giggled.

The brown paper bag between them on the front seat of the car seemed to exert a magnetic force, drawing Robin's eyes to it during the silent car ride back to the cottage. She noticed Patrick's eyes were drawn to it as well. Every time he looked at it, he'd then look at her and smile—a smile so full of promise that Robin could hardly wait to get home so she could take him up on what his eyes were offering.

In the sure knowledge of her love for him, all doubts left her, and she was more ready than she had been even a couple of hours ago. She hadn't thought she'd ever be able to trust again, especially not a reporter, but when she was with Patrick, she didn't think of his occupation at all. Instead, she thought of his gentleness, his wry humor, the way he took care of her.

Discovering she loved Patrick hadn't surprised her; finding she trusted him with her heart did.

She'd known him such a short time—when had it happened? Perhaps it had snuck up on her, the way love had.

When he pulled up in front of the cottage, Robin picked up the paper bag. "The barn or the bed?" she asked softly.

Patrick drew in his breath. "I've got fantasies of making love to you beneath those silly stars on your ceiling and spreading your hair over that slick satin pillowcase."

A smile curved her lips, and Patrick had to remind himself to breathe. It was the smile of a siren, a Lorelei, but even if he'd known it was luring him to his death, he didn't think he could have resisted following that smile inside.

No sooner had she flicked the light on then Patrick had her in his arms. He kissed her again and again, hot, hungry kisses that she took greedily, then gave back. His hand fastened around the rope of hair hanging down her back, sliding off the rubber band that secured it.

"When you wear your hair this way, all I can think about is taking it down." Loosening her hair from its plait, he combed his fingers through it until it hung in silken waves around her shoulders.

Only then did he turn his attention to the sweater she wore. His hands smoothed over the nubby texture, then cupped her breasts before sliding down to lift the sweater up and over her head. Her bra followed, and his hands moved immediately to cover her small, pert breasts.

"Patrick," she moaned breathlessly. "I'm getting a little weak in the knees."

"You're going to be a whole lot weaker before I'm done with you," he growled, then led her over to the bed. He sat her on the edge of it and knelt in front of her to remove her boots, then tugged her back to her feet to remove her jeans and panties.

When she was completely bare, Patrick stood back and just looked at her. Lord, but she was beautiful—small, firm breasts, slim hips, long legs. He reached and gently drew a handful of hair forward over her shoulder and arranged the tangled strands over her breast, so that just her nipple peeked through. "Mine," he whispered through dry lips. "Mine."

Cupping her breasts in his hands, he kissed her until they both trembled with need, then pulled back to fumble with the buttons of his shirt. "Damn," he muttered when his clumsy fingers refused to cooperate.

"Let me." Robin's hands were sure and steady as she undid his buttons one by one. No sooner had she finished than Patrick ripped off the shirt and tossed it carelessly on the floor. He moved his hands to his belt, and Robin laid her hands over his. "No, let me," she said again.

Slow, sweet torture, her hands slid the belt free and dropped it on the floor. She unsnapped the metal snap of his jeans and slid the zipper down, just barely brushing her fingers over the swollen flesh that strained against fabric. Patrick groaned and quickly shed the offending garments, his heavy arousal springing free from its confinement.

A look of hungry absorption on her face, Robin dropped to her knees in front of him, encircling him with her hand and tasting him. Patrick closed his eyes and shuddered, then pulled her to her feet. "If you keep on doing that, we won't get to use the protection we bought." He lay with her on the bed and began loving her in earnest, tasting and savoring every inch of her. As much as he needed to sheathe his aching hardness in her, he needed to do this first.

"Now, Patrick!" Robin pleaded, and when he didn't immediately comply, she curled her fingernails into his shoulders. "Now, please now."

"Now." He agreed, and turned to reach for the protection. It wasn't on the nightstand. He leaned over the side of the bed and looked, but it wasn't on the floor either. He swore briefly, violently.

"On the kitchen counter, I think," she said, her voice tight with need.

Patrick looked at her, lying in his arms, and didn't know if he had the strength to leave her for even a few necessary seconds. He rested his forehead in the little valley between her breasts, feeling the rapid thud of her heart against his cheek. "I could climb a mountain right now to get to you, but I'm not sure I can leave you long enough to get them."

"And I'm not sure I could let you go. But I don't think we have a choice," Robin said softly.

With a look at her that was filled with longing, Patrick got to his feet and hurried to the kitchen. He snared the box, then staggered quickly back to the bed. When Robin rolled on the protection for him, he groaned.

"Oh honey, I want to go slow for you," he murmured, "but I don't know if I can last that long." He waited, poised at the entrance to her body.

"I don't want it slow." Robin took her hand and guided him home.

He groaned as he sank into her slick heat. He'd been right about their fitting together perfectly. He'd also been right that it might drive him insane. When she moved her hips against him, he groaned again. "No, don't, honey, don't move. Just let me breathe a minute." He clutched desperately at his rapidly disintegrating restraint.

"No more waiting, Patrick," Robin vowed, wrapping her legs tightly around him.

Patrick made one last attempt to hold on to reality, then was lost. His world shimmered than shrank until it contained only her and the love he felt for her.

"Patrick?" Her eyes were wide, surprised, as he moved against her.

"Let go, honey, let go."

"I'll fall."

"I'll catch you."

He bent his head to her breasts, lavishing attention on first one tight nipple, then the other. When he felt the spasms that shook her, he took her mouth, swallowing her whimpers of release. Only then did he follow her—joyfully, triumphantly—muffling his shout against her hair. It was not only a physical release, but one of the heart as well.

He collapsed against her, drained but relishing the feeling of her beneath him. It was right— meant to be. He shifted his weight to one side.

"No, don't." Robin tightened her arms around him. "Stay."

"I'm not going anywhere," he breathed, and settled her more securely against him.

Robin nestled her cheek against his shoulder. "I thought you wanted to make love beneath my stars. But you never even turned out the light."

"I'll make love to you beneath your stars later. This time I wouldn't have missed watching you for the world." He levered up on one elbow and painstakingly arranged strands of her hair over the pillow. "That's one fantasy," he said in satisfaction.

"Is it always like this?"

Patrick, who had just laid back down, now propped himself up again. "What?"

"You know"—Robin waved a hand in the air—"like this."

"You mean is it always this good?"

"Yeah. I guess that's what I mean."

"No. It's not. It's never been even half this good for me before."

"It's never been good for me at all."

Patrick smoothed strands of hair away from her face. "You want to tell me about it?"

Robin sighed and stared up at the ceiling. "I was married."

"And?"

"And I was young and inexperienced—a virgin, actually—and, I don't know, it just wasn't very good."

Patrick tensed. "Did he hurt you?"

"No. He was just—it was always over so fast, and then he went to sleep and I lay there wondering if that was all there was."

"So what happened?" Patrick asked casually, though he felt his nerves tighten as he waited for her response. Would she open up to him?

She was silent for so long that he was afraid she wasn't going to answer him at all. Finally, she said, "He—it didn't work out. The marriage was over a year after it started."

"Did you leave him or did he leave you?"

"Enough about me." She feathered her fingers down his chest. "I want to hear about you. Have you ever been seriously involved with anyone else?"

Patrick knew she was trying to change the subject, but he'd let her get away with it . . . this once. "I was married years ago."

"What happened?"

"She had problems when we married, but I was so wrapped up in my first job as a sports reporter, I didn't notice. Of course, she was also a very accomplished liar. I wasn't home often enough, I guess that was part of the problem, but the biggest problem was that she didn't trust me enough to talk to me. If she had, I might have been able to get her some help."

"What was the matter?"

"She was an addict. She died of an overdose two years after we got married."

"That must have been horrible for you."

"It wasn't easy," he agreed. "But the hardest thing of all was knowing that she didn't trust me. Do you trust me, Red?"

Robin slipped a hand down his body. "I trust you as much as I can trust anybody."

Patrick wasn't satisfied with that answer, but he didn't say anything else, seduced into silence by the deliciously wicked things her hands were doing to him.

NINE

They never did get around to making love under the stars, Robin thought when she awoke the next morning in Patrick's arms. Every time she'd tried to extinguish the light, Patrick had turned it back on, saying he'd rather watch her than some ridiculous old stars. She smiled. She hadn't missed the stars either.

She eased herself out of his arms, no easy feat when he kept mumbling, reaching for her, and pulling her back. Swinging her feet out of bed, she almost laughed aloud. They'd forgotten to shut the door all the way, and during the night most of the menagerie had moved inside.

Both cats lay at the head of the bed, next to Patrick's pillow. Chanel was curled up on top of Patrick's discarded jeans, Ritz sat blissfully on the rug in a patch of early morning sun, and Tripod napped at the foot of the bed. Even the dogs, who usually disdained coming inside, had moved to the kitchen floor.

Robin narrowed her eyes in suspicion. They all seemed remarkably well fed for so early in the morning—even Pooh, whose stomach usually woke up at least an hour before Robin's alarm went off. Curious, Robin tugged on her jeans and sweater and went out to the enclosure. Fresh kibble had been put out there as well. The only animals who hadn't already been looked after were the baby squirrels and a syringe, can of puppy formula, and can opener lay ready on the table.

Patrick's thoughtfulness gave her a warm glow deep down inside, even where that so-carefully-protected core of hers had lain frozen for the last few years. And as it melted, it filled her up so much inside, she didn't know if she could hold all the love she felt.

A silly grin pasted itself on her face as she filled a syringe with formula and removed a baby squirrel from its cage. She absently held the wriggling creature as it suckled. Years from now, she mused fancifully, maybe they'd find her staring off dreamily into space with that same stupid grin on her face.

When the last baby had been fed and a couple

of dressings changed, she hurried back inside the house. Patrick was still asleep, her pillow clutched to him as if he'd reached out for her again and found that instead. Robin felt her heart beat faster at just the sight of him.

How had she fallen in love with him in such a phenomenally short period of time? And why, after knowing John Douglas a year before she'd married him, had she not felt this intensity? She sat on the edge of the bed, tracing her fingers down Patrick's cheek. She didn't know if he'd want to hear her say it, but she thought he was the most beautiful man she'd ever met. She sighed. He'd probably already been told that more than once.

She decided to go all out for breakfast this morning, fixing her grandma's steamed raisin-walnut oatmeal. She put the oatmeal on to simmer, chopped the walnuts, mixed the cinnamon and brown sugar topping, then turned back to stir the oatmeal. When an arm slipped around her waist from behind, she was startled for a moment, then leaned back against Patrick's warm body.

"Mmm, something smells good," he murmured in her ear.

"Cinnamon and brown sugar?"

"No, it's you." He buried his face in her hair. Robin turned in his embrace and hooked her arms around his neck, feeling just a little bit shy. She'd had only one other lover in her life—and she'd been married to him—so she wasn't exactly sure of the etiquette following a night of wild passion. Not that she'd ever had such a night with John Douglas anyway. "Good morning."

"It is that," Patrick agreed, and slid his hands under her sweater, where he encountered the smooth skin of her back and nothing else. "You're not wearing a bra."

She tilted her head to one side. "So I'm not," she agreed.

Patrick slid his hands down over her buttocks. "What else are you not wearing?"

"That's for me to know and you—"

"To find out!" Patrick's hands unsnapped the waist of her jeans. "And I intend to do just that."

"Later," she said primly, hiding a smile as she turned toward the stove. "I have to finish breakfast, but just to ease your curiosity. I'm wearing panties."

Patrick sighed. "Well then, I'll just sit here at the table and watch you."

Robin went on as if she hadn't heard. "Pink satin panties. The ones that match the camisole that so intrigued you."

Before she even had a chance to set down the spoon, she wound up flat on her back on the bed, with her jeans around her ankles. "Pink satin," Patrick murmured in satisfaction, as he ran his hands over them. "Another fantasy."

"How many fantasies do you have?"

"About you? Dozens, hundreds, maybe thousands."

"You haven't known me long enough to have thousands." Her voice caught as he slipped his fingers inside the slick pink fabric.

"Maybe not, but I've known you long enough to fall in love with you."

Another silly grin spread over her face. "You love me?"

"Head over heels."

"I love you too."

Robin watched as a matching grin covered his face, just before he wrapped his arms around her and held her as though he couldn't get close enough. Things got a little hazy after that as they explored each other with the eyes and hands of new love. By the time they finally made it to the kitchen table, the oatmeal had long since cooked to a charred glutinous lump.

Robin watched Patrick as he ate his second ham-and-cheese sandwich. "Are there any other fantasies besides pink satin I should be aware of?" she asked.

An unholy gleam lit Patrick's eyes, and he

tossed the remainder of his sandwich on the table.
"Let's go back to bed, and I'll describe a few."

"I have some babies to feed," Robin said wistfully. "Will you show me later?"

"With infinite pleasure and in great detail."

Patrick followed her around the enclosure asking question after question—both serious and nonsensical. He helped out when he could and, when he couldn't, sat watching her with hungry eyes. As soon as she tucked the last baby in, she turned to Patrick and said, "Now about those fantasies—"

They made love again, this time on the old army blanket on the pile of straw in the barn. Later, Robin lay cuddled against him, wrapped in his arms and nothing else. Even though he was sated and satisfied, Patrick couldn't keep his hands off her—stroking her hair, her arm, her breast. He just knew he needed to stay connected with her in some way.

He stared at the dust motes dancing in the ray of late-afternoon sun that had found its way in through a tiny crack in the wall. He loved her and she loved him, but he couldn't rest easy until all the secrets between them had been broached. Secrets could fester and destroy the person keeping them, and he'd never let that happen to Robin. But even more than wanting to keep her safe, he simply wanted her complete trust. More, he needed it.

Settling her head more comfortably against his shoulder, he dropped a kiss on her hair. "Tell me about your husband, Red."

Silence. Patrick forced his body to stay relaxed, not wanting her to know just how important it was to him that she answer.

Finally, slowly, she replied. "We met in college. I was nineteen. We married six months later, on my twentieth birthday."

"You were young."

"Much too young," she agreed. "I was old money, he was new. Do you know what I mean?" She raised her head to look at Patrick.

"I'm not sure. Tell me."

"My family was old, established, affluent— well, up until Daddy lost most of it in a couple of bad investments. But you know the trappings— tasteful home, tasteful cars, tasteful clothes, tasteful friends. John Douglas was new money— huge, lush house, fancy cars, all the rest. He was so different from anyone else I knew—flashy, larger-than-life. He called me his princess. He even gave me a diamond tiara to wear on our wedding day. . . ." Her voice trailed off, and she laid her head back on Patrick's chest.

"Were you happy?" His voice rumbled beneath her ear.

"For a month or two, maybe. I don't know. I thought I was, anyway." Her fingers absently traced circles in the hair on his chest. "But I knew something wasn't right. There were too many unexplained absences. Too many so-called meetings late at night with his brother, and I was too stupid to figure it all out. I mean, he supposedly was in an import/export business. How many late-night meetings did they have to have?"

"So what happened, honey?" He laid his hand over hers.

"He and Malcolm had a horrible argument, and I couldn't stand it, so I went over to my mother's for a while," she murmured. "When I came home a couple of hours later, he was dead. Apparently a suicide, though I've often wondered whether Malcolm . . ." Her voice trailed off.

Suicide! "That must have been very difficult for you," he said carefully.

"A widow before I was even twenty-one."

"Why did he commit suicide?" When she stirred restlessly, Patrick began stroking her hair, petting her like a cat. She relaxed against him for a moment, then rolled over and sat, pulling her knees up and wrapping her arms around them.

She trusted him. She did, but it was so hard to

make the words come out. "H-he found out he was under investigation by the federal government for smuggling. He just couldn't handle it, I guess."

"I see. He was guilty." The words were matter-of-fact.

"As sin."

"So what happened then?" Patrick asked quietly, sitting up behind her.

"Then the government came in and confiscated all his property—even the things I'd brought with me when we got married. Illegally gotten goods, they said, and the insurance company said, 'Sorry, it's a suicide—no money.' I went from designer dresses to discount jeans in just a couple of weeks."

Patrick wrapped his arms around her and tugged her back to lean against him. "What happened to his brother?"

"He skipped town with all the money in the business checking account—they've recently picked him up and shipped him back to Norfolk to stand trial."

"The reporters—they figure in this somewhere, don't they?"

Robin nodded. "They hounded me mercilessly for a story—they wanted all the gory details. 'The Princess and the Bad Boy,' they kept calling us. I was young, still fairly naive, and terribly confused. I said some things and made some of the press hate me." For a moment she stopped, awash in memories. Taking a deep breath, she shook them away.

"Next thing I knew, they were intimating that I'd known about John Douglas's activities and kept my mouth shut because I liked the money. The worst, though, was the rumor that, not only had I known about everything, but that I actively participated."

"But you didn't."

"Is that a statement, or are you looking for an affirmation?"

"Robin!" Hurt colored his voice.

"Sorry." She turned and hugged him, laying her head against his shoulder. "Old habits die hard, I guess."

"So tell me the rest."

"They just wouldn't let up, Patrick. By the time they were done, I'd lost my job, and the friends who'd taken me in kicked me back out. I stayed in a seedy little motel for a few weeks, hoping things would die down and I could get on with my life. That all changed when an old friend drove me home one evening, told me to keep my chin up, and gave me a hug."

"A male friend," guessed Patrick.

"Just a friend, but the press took a picture of that, and next day it appeared in the paper with a caption saying the Princess hadn't wasted any time after the death of her husband. The final straw was when they suggested that maybe John Douglas's death hadn't been a suicide after all. The day after the article appeared, I packed up what few belongings I had and left Norfolk for good."

He cradled her against him. "God, no wonder you didn't like or trust reporters. I'm sorry, honey."

She shook her head, her silky curls caressing his chest as she did. "Don't apologize—you didn't do anything. And, to be honest, it was only a few who worked for less than reputable papers who did it all."

"What exactly was it your husband had done?" Patrick's hand absently tangled in her hair, rubbing it between his fingers.

"He and his brother had been smuggling in the furs of endangered species."

A light dawned, and he pushed her far enough away to see her face. "That's why you're so interested in educating the public about endangered animals, isn't it? You feel you have to make some sort of reparations."

Robin shook her head. "No. I felt that way in

the beginning, I guess, but now I genuinely believe it's the right thing to do, and I truly love what I do here."

Patrick didn't doubt that for a minute. He'd seen her face when she went about her sometimes grueling, always time-consuming routine. "How did you wind up in Needle Ridge?" He pulled her back to him.

"One of the things Daddy left me when he died, besides a small monthly allowance, was the deed to this cabin. When I was young, we'd come here a few times each summer. Daddy would go fishing, Mom would catch up on her sleep, and I'd ride my bike into town and play with a little girl named Maggie Grinstead."

"Marge?"

Patrick could feel her smile against his shoulder.

"Yeah. She always hated being called Maggie, so I started calling her Marge."

"So you came here to escape and . . . ?"

"Marge introduced me to Joey—he'd just started the clinic—and he gave me a job as a veterinary assistant. People were always bringing in baby animals like birds or squirrels or something, and I started taking them home with me over the weekend.

"Then Joey and I came up with the idea of

keeping the occasional wild animal here. It was quieter than the clinic—no dogs barking, cats meowing, kids running in and out—and the animals seemed to do better. He worked with me on getting my rehabilitator's license, and from there it was a short step to this."

Patrick hugged her tightly. She'd walked through fire in her life, but like tempered steel, had become stronger for it. "I love you," he whispered, and kissed her.

The last little remnant of mistrust melted completely, and she returned his kiss with every particle of her being. A man to believe in, she thought foggily, as he pushed her back onto the blanket. She'd finally found a man to believe in.

They were eating a late supper when the telephone rang. Robin laughingly rose from her perch on Patrick's lap and grabbed it.

"Hello?" The smile on her face faded, to be replaced with a look of wariness. Her eyes locked with Patrick's. "No, you didn't interrupt anything . . . Richmond? Yes, I can be there Friday." A huge smile broke over her face. "Thank you, Mrs. Russell. Thank you so much." She slowly hung up the phone, her hand lingering over it as if she wanted to make sure it was real.

Patrick came up behind her, and she spun around and threw herself into his arms. "I did it! I did it!"

"Did what?"

"Got the grant. Well, it's not official for sure, I mean, I have to go to Richmond on Friday and meet the director, but they're very impressed with my ideas, and she, that's Mrs. Russell, said I'm definitely the first choice and—oh, I need to call Joey, and . . ."

Patrick listened to her excited rambling and mentally said a prayer of thanks. She looked like a child who'd just been given the keys to Disneyland. "We need to celebrate, honey. Tell you what, you call Joey and Marge and invite them over. I'm going to make a quick dash into town." He grabbed her Jeep keys off the kitchen counter and gave her a quick but thorough kiss. "Dress for the occasion," he murmured against her mouth. "I have a real urge to see your legs."

When Patrick returned, Joey, Marge, and Betsy were already there. He gave a quick hug to Marge and Betsy, but his eyes were all for Robin. He'd hoped she'd wear a dress, but he had no complaints with the slim knit trousers and white sweater she wore.

The black trousers clung lovingly to her hips, and the sweater—well, the sweater was guaranteed to keep a man awake at night. It was a thin lacy knit cut low over the bosom. Through a band of open lace weave down the front, he could see the barest tinge of pink, and he had a sudden urge to rip that sweater right off to see if she was indeed wearing that wicked pink satin camisole.

"Hey, you cleaned up real good," was all he said as he handed her a bottle of champagne.

They sat and talked and drank champagne until Betsy, who'd been in the shelter playing with Tripod and the cats, came inside and yawned and reminded her parents that she had to leave an hour early in the morning for a school trip. She hugged Robin and offered to help take care of the animals over the weekend if Robin wanted to stay in Richmond a day or two extra. "You know," she said shyly, "you and Uncle Trick would make a totally awesome couple."

"Thank you, Miss Matchmaker," Marge said, and looped an arm around her preteen daughter's shoulder. "Let's go." As she went out the door, she turned back and grinned. "Personally, I think Betsy's got great instincts."

Patrick waved good-bye, then shut the door. "Do you think Betsy's got great instincts?"

"On the money," Robin murmured. "Though I'm awesome and you're just totally."

"Totally what?" Patrick traced his finger around the scoop neck of her sweater.

Robin caught her breath when his finger slipped beneath the neck. "Totally sexy."

"I was a little disappointed at not seeing you in a dress, but I'm getting over it." His eyes darkened. "What do you have on underneath that sweater?"

"Guess!"

"I'm not into guessing games, Red. I prefer hide-and-seek myself, and I've a real strong urge to seek what you're hiding." He tugged the sweater over her head and tossed it on the kitchen table, just missing the half-empty bowl of popcorn they'd been munching. He groaned. "Pink satin. I just knew it. You don't know how close you came to having your clothes ripped off earlier."

"What's the fascination with pink satin?" Robin said breathlessly, as he bent and flicked his tongue over the nipple outlined by the slick fabric.

"I don't know. For some reason even the thought of it makes me want to get you out of it as soon as possible." He grasped the spaghetti straps and drew the camisole down her arms, baring her breasts.

"Just as well I didn't wear my pink satin

blouse, isn't it?" She gasped as he lifted her into his arms and set her on the edge of the kitchen table.

"Now for another fantasy."

The meeting on Friday went perfectly, and Robin was offered the grant money. She'd also taken Betsy up on her offer and spent a romantic weekend away with Patrick. By Monday, she felt she'd never been happier in her life.

She and Patrick slept late Monday morning, having gotten in late the night before and then gotten to sleep even later because of their love-making. Of course, Robin's idea of sleeping late was waking up early to tend the animals, then crawling sleepily back into Patrick's arms to doze another hour or two.

The shrill ring of the telephone woke her, and she stumbled to the kitchen. "H'lo?" She stifled a yawn.

"Miss McKenna?"

"Yes, this is Robin McKenna."

"Miss McKenna, I'm Daniel Foster, legal representative for the Webster Foundation."

"Yes, Mr. Foster."

"I'm afraid that in view of information that has recently come to light, the foundation must withdraw the grant funding. We must have no hint of scandal attached to the organization."

"I beg your pardon?" Robin said stupidly.

"Please understand, Miss McKenna, this is in no way an indictment of your guilt or innocence, and we sincerely apologize for any inconvenience caused you, but as a small private foundation, we are extremely strict."

"Mr. Foster, I'm afraid I have no idea what you're talking about."

"Miss McKenna." The voice held a thread of impatience. "Surely you realize that we simply cannot ignore the information that came to light in yesterday's newspaper article. Again we apologize for any inconvenience. Good day."

"Mr. Foster?" But the connection was broken. What newspaper, she wanted to ask. She supposed he meant the Richmond Sunday paper, but how could she be sure? Robin continued to stare at the silent phone for long moments, as if the instrument itself could give her the answers she needed.

"Robin?" Patrick murmured from the bed. "What's going on?"

"I don't know." She gave a short laugh. "The Webster Foundation has rescinded the grant, and I don't even know what I did."

With one lithe movement Patrick tossed back

the covers and got to his feet. In three strides he was beside her, his hands on her shoulders. "What did he say, honey?"

Robin's brow knit in thought. "He said they couldn't allow any hint of scandal to touch the foundation and then said this was not an indictment of my guilt or innocence. What guilt or innocence?" She turned stricken eyes to Patrick. "What in the world do they think I've done?"

Patrick pulled her into his arms and held her. "Was that all he said?"

"No, he said something about an article in the newspaper. What newspaper? He must mean the Richmond Sunday paper, but why would they have an article about me?"

"One way to find out. Does the bookstore carry copies of the Richmond paper?"

"I'm sure they do. There are several vending machines around that do, too, but they wouldn't still have yesterday's paper."

"That's why we'll check the bookstore. They probably would."

Robin nodded and brightened. Maybe once she'd read the article, she'd know how to fight back. After all, she hadn't done anything. "I'm sure it's a misunderstanding of some sort, but I've just got to have that grant money."

Patrick pulled her to sit next to him on the

bed. "I know it would help, but if you don't get it, at least you can continue to do what you're doing and wait for the next chance." He looked at her face, the set jaw, the lowered eyes. "Can't you?"

Slowly, she shook her head. "I had to turn animals away last spring, Patrick. Dozens of them. I didn't have enough room, enough cages, or enough food. Joey ended up having to put down wild animals that could have been rehabilitated had there been a place to keep them."

"What about the wildlife center you've been dealing with?"

"They're as crowded as I am. Why do you think they keep bringing their overflow to me? I've been dipping into my savings just to make ends meet. The income from Daddy just barely covers my living expenses here—that's not counting things like food for the animals, cages, supplies. And it doesn't cover the new roof or the new heating unit I need to have put in the shelter before next winter, and it doesn't cover the twenty-year-old hot-water heater that's going to give up the ghost any day now."

Robin sighed heavily. "Patrick, there are so many things that need doing, and I can't afford any of them. But this is all a mistake. I know it is. Everything will be all right once I know what they're talking about."

Patrick opened his mouth to offer his own money, then thought of the balance of his savings account. He was successful in his field, but unfortunately his field wasn't one in which you got rich. He simply tightened his arms around her and silently vowed to do whatever he could to get her those funds.

"I'm going into town to get a paper," Robin declared. "I'll drop you off by Dr. Martin's on the way. He wanted to look at your ankle one more time, didn't he?"

"I think I should go with you."

Robin hugged him. "I'll be fine. I even promise not to jump up and down and scream in the bookstore. I just need to check out the article and find out what misconceptions the foundation might have, that's all."

"But I don't have an appointment with Dr. Martin."

"Small Town America, remember?"

They dressed, and Robin drove into town, dropping Patrick off at the doctor's office, which happened to be a converted garage attached to his house. Robin then drove straight to Bibi's Bookstore and went straight to the shelves with newspapers from all over the eastern United States. There was one Richmond paper left from yesterday and Robin grabbed it, then sat at the table provided.

She scanned one section after another before finding the article, then skimmed it quickly. "The Webster Foundation's grant for the enhancement and protection of wildlife has been offered this year to Miss Robin McKenna of Needle Ridge. Miss McKenna, formerly known as Teresa Exbury, was married to the late John Douglas Exbury, who was involved in . . . now resides in the northwest part of the state, and we were unable to reach her for comment. . . ."

It was a straightforward article, no implications or innuendos, just a simple accounting of the facts. It was all here—that she'd been suspected of having had knowledge of, and perhaps participation in, her husband's activities, even the fact that she'd briefly been under suspicion of murder. Even though it started emphatically that the suspicions had been groundless and that she had been cleared, the facts looked so damaging in print.

Robin winced, sighed, then crumpled the paper in her hands. "Well," she murmured, "at least I know why the foundation backed off. Five years later and reporters are still ruining my life. Why couldn't he just let it be?"

The man sitting across from her eyed her

strangely but said nothing as she dropped the paper on the table and left, tossing a couple of dollars on the counter on her way out.

One thing puzzled her. Five years ago she'd had her name changed—quietly and legally. How had this reporter—this Bill Marsh character—made the connection? He may have ruined her life, but, by George, she was going to find out how.

That decision made, she dropped by the clinic on the way to pick up Patrick and asked Joey if she could use his phone. She placed a call to the newspaper office and asked if there was any way she could get in touch with Bill Marsh. To her surprise he was there and came to the phone.

"Mr. Marsh? This is Robin McKenna. I read your article."

"Oh, nice to hear from you. Congratulations on being awarded the grant. Did you like the article?"

"Oh, yes," she lied smoothly. "Um, Mr. Marsh, I was just curious as to how you made the connection between me and my old life. I've tried very hard to start over. I'm sure you can understand."

"Oh, I do. That's why I thought it made a great human-interest story."

"How *did* you make the connection?"

"Now you know we don't usually disclose our sources, but since it was a friend of yours, I don't suppose it would matter."

"A friend of mine?"

"Yeah, Trick Brady." Her suddenly nerveless fingers dropped the phone. And she fell, more than leaned, against the wall. *Patrick?* This was Patrick's doing?

TEN

"Hey, Robin?" Joey poked his head in his office. "Good Lord! Are you all right?" He dashed to her side.

"No," she said dully. "I'm sick, Joey. Sick to my very heart."

Joey pulled up a chair and made her sit, then handed her the soda he'd been about to drink. "What's wrong?"

Robin stared blindly across the room. "When am I ever going to learn? You'd think that I'd have learned by now, wouldn't you?"

"Drink the soda, then tell me what happened."

Robin took a halfhearted sip, then told Joey everything.

"I can't believe Trick would do something

like this." Joey shook his head. "He just wouldn't."

"Why wouldn't he?" she cried out bitterly. "He's a reporter. It's the story of my life, Joey. What do I have to do to get away from the past? I keep running and running, and it just keeps finding me."

"Where's Trick?"

"Dr. Martin's."

"You've got to talk to him, Robin. Everything will be all right, I know it. There has to be an explanation. He wouldn't do something like this. I know he wouldn't."

"I'm going to lose everything. I was counting on that grant money. I might be able to manage through the summer, but without that new heating system in the shelter, I won't be able to go over the winter. I guess it wasn't meant to be. Maybe I should just give up and—"

"Absolutely not! Things will work out. I know they will. Just hang in there. And, please, talk to Trick."

"I don't think I can right now." Robin swallowed the sobs that burned the back of her throat. "I need to go home." Vaguely, she wondered if she sounded the way she felt—like a little girl who desperately needed her mother.

"What about Patrick?"

"I—I just can't deal with him right now. You can pick up his clothes later. They'll be on the porch."

"Robin—"

Spinning on her heel, she left, and sat in her car for a long time before she felt steady enough to drive. But she forced herself not to cry. This pain went too deep for tears. The anguish, the feeling of betrayal, seemed rooted in her very heart.

When she got home, she scooped up Patrick's things and stuffed them into his suitcase, then found herself stroking trembling fingers over the rumpled sweatshirt lying on the foot of the bed. She remembered tugging it over his head last night and tossing it aside. Clenching her hand around it, she snatched it up and stuffed it in his bag as well, resisting the urge to bury her face in the soft fleece. Grabbing the rest of his things, she piled them into the porch swing, went inside, and shut the door.

When Patrick climbed out of Dr. Martin's car, he saw his things piled in the swing and stopped in his tracks. What in the world was going on?

"Robin?" He tried the screen door, but it was

locked. "Robin, what's going on?" She didn't answer, so he knocked loudly. "Robin?"

When she still didn't answer, he banged the door with his fist. "For God's sake, Robin! Open the door. Please. Is something wrong?"

What the hell had set her off? He kicked the door in frustration. "I can stay here all day, if you like. You have to come out sometime to feed the animals. I'll wait." With that, he dumped his stuff out of the swing and sat down, crossing his arms, confusion and frustration turning in him like a windmill.

He hadn't waited more than two or three minutes when he heard Robin's voice through the door. "Why don't you just leave? Haven't you done enough damage?"

Patrick leapt to his feet and stood right next to the door. "I don't understand, honey, what have I done?"

"Joey didn't tell you?"

"I haven't seen Joey. Dr. Martin dropped me off. Please talk to me, Robin. Tell me what happened."

The door opened, and Robin stepped outside. Her eyes were as cold a gold-green as he'd ever seen, and her arms were crossed protectively in front of her. "I just want to know why you did it.

I opened my home to you, and yet you couldn't wait to get a story out of it."

"I don't know what you're talking about, Robin. I swear I don't. I would never do anything to hurt you. I love you."

She turned her back to him, but not before he saw the agony that glittered in her eyes. "Don't say that again," she muttered tightly. "Don't ever say that again. I talked to your friend, Patrick."

Confused, baffled, totally in the dark—none of them completely described how lost Patrick felt. "What friend?"

"The one who wrote the article that destroyed my life," she said bitterly. "The one who said he got his information from you."

"I don't understand. Who?"

"Does the name Bill Marsh mean anything to you?" Her tears under at least temporary control, she turned back just in time to see Patrick blanch. "I can see it does."

"He was the one who wrote the story? He's never indulged in yellow journalism before. For God's sake, what in the world did he say?"

"Oh, he didn't have to make up anything. All he had to do was connect the names Robin McKenna and Teresa Robin Exbury, and the damage took care of itself." Her voice was husky with both anger and pain. "And he made that connection because of you. Can you deny it?"

"Oh, hell. Robin, it wasn't like that. I called Bill the second night I was here. I don't know why. I'd just found the clipping in your nightstand drawer, and—" *I was just curious?* Patrick's heart sank. No matter what his reasons at the time, now they sounded damning.

"What clipping?"

Patrick took a deep breath before saying, "The one where you're leaving your husband's funeral."

"All this time, you've known?" A wave of illness hit Robin, and she thought she might throw up. He'd known! That night when he'd come up to the loft and been so sweet, he'd known. When she'd lain naked in his arms and talked about her disastrous marriage, he'd known.

He closed his eyes for a moment, then opened them again, and gazed at her in agony. "I didn't know everything, but I figured out some both from the clipping and the news on the radio."

"Why did you do it, Patrick?" She wanted to sound accusatory; instead, she just sounded miserable.

Patrick ran a hand through his hair, then shook his head slightly. "God, I don't know, Robin. I was fascinated by you, even from the beginning. Hell, maybe I was in love with you even then. I wanted to know everything about you. It seemed innocent enough at the time. And I never intended any of this to happen. You've got to believe me, honey."

"Why?" She felt tired. So tired. "Why do I have to believe you?"

"Because you love me. I love you," he said desperately.

"Do you? Do I? I don't know anymore. Can I love a man who ruins my life? I thought I loved my husband, and he ruined me. And now you."

He flinched. "I'll make things right somehow, honey. I promise you I will." He reached out a hand to her, but she shied away. At her instinctive response, he felt as if he'd been kicked in the gut. He stepped toward her.

"Why can't you trust me?" His words were more a plea than a question. Dear Lord, it was all falling apart, and he didn't know how to stop it.

She backed away a few steps and whispered, "Because I don't know you."

He clenched his fists at his side. "Somehow, someway. I'm going to make things right. Mark my words. I love you, and I'll do whatever I have to do."

Grabbing his suitcase off the porch, he started to leave, but turned back just in time to see

Robin's face crumple into tears. When he took a step toward her, she shut the door.

Patrick stared at the door for endless moments, taking deep breaths and trying to steady the trembling of his hands. For a few brief moments, his life had been so perfect. And now it had all been ripped apart. Eyes burning, he sighed heavily and turned away.

ELEVEN

Spring in the mountains was green and fresh, and the sounds were gentle—birds staking out their territory, the rustle of animals foraging for their young, the whisper of wind through the newly leafed-out branches. Spring in the city was hardly noticeable—the green camouflaged by concrete and car fumes, the sounds masked by engines, telephones, and boom boxes. Patrick missed spring.

But not as much as he missed Robin. The aching void inside him stayed there no matter where he went or what he did. And he did plenty. But no matter how busy he stayed, he was never too busy to hurt.

His eyes searched through every crowd looking for her impossibly tangled hair and impudent smile, only he never found them. At night he held his pillow next to him, but somehow it served only to point out the emptiness in his arms.

He tried everything he could think of, from hounding the insurance company to talking to the police about Malcolm Exbury's involvement in his brother's death, but found only dead ends. After a fruitless confrontation with the Webster Foundation, he came home to find his twin brother, Jason, sprawled on his sofa.

"Whoa! You look terrible, Trick."

"Thanks. What're you doing here? I thought you were in Seattle."

"That job's over. I'm heading to Panama next. I'll be gone about six weeks. I had a feeling that I ought to come by, though. You want to talk about it?"

Patrick sighed with frustration. "May as well." He told Jason all about Robin and about what he'd done, however innocently, to hurt her. "I'm at a loss, Jason. I just don't know what to do."

"Well"—Jason took a swig from his lukewarm soft drink—"I think you should do what you do best. Write." He glanced at his watch. "Oops, gotta go. My flight leaves in about an hour. I'll see you when I get back."

Patrick paced the floor most of the night, thinking about what Jason had said. Finally, toward dawn, he sat down at his typewriter and wrote about Robin. He poured his heart out on paper, trying to show Robin as he saw her—a strong, caring, idealistic young woman who was trying to make a difference, despite financial difficulties and a tragic past.

He took the article to his editor the next morning, before he could change his mind. After all that had happened between himself and Robin, the article couldn't do anymore damage and might even help a little. He hoped. He tried to ignore the clench of desperation in his gut.

Tomorrow, he'd drive to Needle Ridge with two dozen roses, a case of puppy formula, and two 50-pound bags of kibble in tow. Not that he was trying to bribe her, but it couldn't hurt. After all, he'd called her twice a day for the past two and a half weeks, and she'd hung up on him every time. Please, God, he prayed silently. Please let her listen to me. Please let her still love me.

It was late when he finally arrived at the cabin. The lights were out and the door locked, but Patrick made a beeline through the enclosure to the fenced backyard. The window next to the bed was opened slightly, so he quietly raised it farther and climbed inside.

Robin lay sleeping beneath her glowing stars, and Patrick's heart turned over. This was where he belonged. Didn't she realize that? He quietly undressed, leaving on his jeans, and got into bed next to her, pulling her into his arms. When she murmured and nestled closer, he sighed shakily and tightened his embrace. He lay awake long into the night, afraid of what her reaction might be when she awoke and saw him, yet comforted by her nearness.

"Patrick? Get up!"

"Mmph."

"I said, get up! Why are you here?"

Patrick struggled to a sitting position, and Robin ran her eyes over him. Why did he still look so good to her? She wanted to throw herself back into his arms and never let go, but she clenched her hands on the arms of the rocking chair instead.

"I came to see you."

Had he noticed the dark circles beneath her eyes that hadn't been there before? Could he tell she'd lost about six pounds she couldn't afford to lose? She instinctively garnered all her defenses. He wouldn't get the chance to cause her any more pain. "It's a long drive." Thankfully she sounded cool and polite.

Patrick shrugged and smiled, but the smile never reached his shadowed eyes. "I brought roses, but I left them in the car. They're probably wilted by now. I also brought a case of puppy formula and a couple bags of kibble. I left them just inside the enclosure. Are you okay?"

"Fine." She smiled a brittle smile that felt as if it would crack and break any minute. "Everything's fine. How about you?"

"Miserable. Everything's miserable. I miss you." He didn't make a move toward her, but his eyes reached out to her with a gaze that was almost tangible in its intensity.

"Patrick—" She took a step back, needing distance.

"The animals?"

"They're fine. Look, I have a pretty full day ahead. . . ." *Please*, she pleaded silently, *please just leave me alone.*

"Tell me the truth, Robin. I can tell by looking at you that something's wrong."

Robin pushed her hair out of her face with an impatient hand. "Okay, you want it? You got it," she snapped. "The hot-water heater blew two days ago, and when they came in to look at it, they found all the plumbing except the shower needs to be replaced. I can't afford it. All the cages are full, and I've had to send the overflow to Joey to keep as long as he has the space. I don't have it."

She looked at him with shuttered eyes. "I have

a real estate agent coming over tomorrow. I'm going to sell the cabin."

"No!" He jumped to his feet. "Don't do it, honey. Everything will be all right. I promise.

"Don't do anything yet!" He grabbed her by the shoulders. "Promise me." When she didn't answer, he gave her an urgent shake. "Promise me."

She pulled away and turned around, hugging herself as if she were cold. "All right. I'll postpone the meeting with the realtor until Friday, but no longer. I can't wait forever. I can't afford to. Now would you just go?"

Patrick turned her around, dropped a kiss on her lips, and left. His heart ached as he drove, each mile farther away only increasing the intensity of the pain. He felt . . . homeless. And scared. He was rapidly running out of options. The only thing he hadn't tried was applying for the largest loan the bank would give him. He owned his apartment; maybe they'd let him use that as collateral. If that didn't work, he'd think of something else. He'd have to. He couldn't give up on her. And he couldn't let her give up on her dream.

Funny, Robin mused as she stared out over the meadow, how her work seemed so ordinary now. She'd lost all of her joy in it. Was it because she knew she would lose it all soon? No, her heart admitted, even though her head didn't want to acknowledge it, it was because Patrick wasn't there. Her beautiful green mountain, brilliant blue sky, and artist's palette of spring flowers seemed all shades of gray because Patrick wasn't there to see them with her.

Even the animals seemed to miss him. Ritz wandered aimlessly around, flapping his one wing and quacking softly to himself, and Pooh sat and watched Robin intently, as if wanting to know where Robin had put Patrick.

How could she still love a man who had betrayed her? Or *had* he? She'd gone over and over this in her head a dozen times—a hundred times—and she still wasn't sure. He did love her—she couldn't deny that. A memory of the stark hunger and pain in his eyes still haunted her.

The ever-present ache and confusion were like living things inside her—twisting and turning and rushing forward at the slightest provocation, causing Robin to bite her lip and forcibly blink back the tears.

Would she ever be free of the ache? she wondered, when she went to get her afternoon's mail. Her heart beat a little faster as she saw an envelope with handwriting on the outside. Patrick?

Her heart sank when she saw it wasn't from him, but she found herself staring in surprise. There were two envelopes with checks in them. One had a note saying this was for her good work and to keep it up. The other had no note at all, except for a notation at the bottom of the check that said "for animals." Neither check was very large, twenty-five and ten dollars respectively, but considering Robin hadn't been expecting either of them, she was surprised.

The next day six checks came in the mail, five of them in the twenty- to thirty-dollar range, one for two hundred dollars. Again, the notes simply said to keep up the good work—the ones that contained notes.

Puzzled, she called Joey and asked if he knew anything about it. From the way he hesitated, she figured he did. "Come on, spit it out, Joey."

"Well, this is the work of one of those damned reporters."

She shivered. "Patrick?"

"He wrote a feature article about you last week for the paper. It was a wonderful article, and a lot of people have apparently been moved to contribute something to your wildlife center."

"But—but I have no wildlife center."

"Yet."

The next day brought more contributions—

from a crumpled dollar bill to a check for five hundred dollars. She was still sorting through her mail with a bemused expression on her face when Joey stopped by.

"Joey, look at all this. I don't believe it."

"Then you really won't believe this." He handed her a large brown envelope bulging with dozens of checks. "This was just delivered to me from the newspaper office. These had all been sent there for you. There's even a pledge in here from a prominent family for ten thousand dollars a year for ten years."

"Oh, my God."

"I guess this is one time a reporter hasn't messed up your life, hmm?" Joey's words were pointed.

"Oh, Joey," she sighed. "It's not that he's a reporter." That was true, she realized in some surprise. That he was a reporter didn't bother her at all. "It's that he—he ruined everything. How could I ever trust him again not to do the same thing?"

"By growing up," Joey said succinctly, and left.

Robin tossed her shoes at the door, then stalked into the bathroom to take a shower. Darn him, anyway! She wasn't sure just whom she was mad at, though—Joey, for making her feel like a child in a snit, or Patrick, for making her feel— making her feel confused? Frustrated? Lonely? Miserable?

Yes, she was miserable. And she looked terrible to prove it. The bags beneath her eyes had bags, and if she lost any more weight, her jeans would start falling down. She really missed him. But how *could* she trust him again? She stared at her reflection in the mirror.

"I can't eat, I can't sleep, and I'm tried of soggy pillows," she murmured. "So what am I going to do about it?" Ritz, who stood in the little puddle left in the shower, let out a solitary quack.

She asked herself that question a lot over the next few days. Her money worries apparently over, she had a lot of time to think and spent most of it thinking about Patrick. He had told her he'd make things right somehow, and he had. That made up for the problems he'd inadvertently caused. Didn't it? He'd kept his word, something John Douglas had never done. And somehow she knew he'd keep his word about other important things too. Things like vows of love.

She sat on her front porch swing, staring out into space, but seeing only Patrick's face. Those sweet-syrup eyes, that determined jaw, those lips that could bring her so much pleasure.

"How's it going?"

Robin looked up at Joey, not at all surprised to see him there. It seemed like fate to her. "I think I'm growing up, Joey. Do you think he'll ever want to see me again?"

"I don't think that's a problem. Should I send Marge to help you pack?"

"I'm hoping clothes won't be necessary."

"Robin!"

"Grow up, Joey."

Robin changed clothes, putting on newer jeans and a pink satin blouse. She brushed her unruly hair until it haloed in a soft cloud around her shoulders and even applied a little makeup— something she seldom bothered with. Grabbing her purse, she jumped in the Jeep. She only hoped her sweaty palms could keep a grip on the steering wheel.

When she finally arrived in Washington, D.C., she wound up lost for several hours but eventually found Patrick's apartment building. It was in a nice neighborhood with a decidedly preppie flavor—the kind of neighborhood she'd cut her teeth on as a child. She went inside and climbed to the second floor. Patrick wasn't home, but she hadn't expected him to be in the middle of the afternoon. She sat on the landing and stretched out her legs. However long it took, she'd wait.

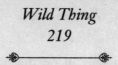

When Patrick pulled up in front of the cabin, Joey's car was there but not Robin's Jeep. Was something wrong? He checked the house first, then the enclosure. There he found Marge feeding a baby squirrel. "Where's Robin?"

Marge glanced up, and a look of horror passed over her face. "What are you doing here, Patrick? Go home."

"Where's Robin?"

"She's not here."

"I'll wait."

"She's not going to be here for a while, Patrick. I think you should go home and come back later."

"Marge, D.C.'s not exactly around the block. It's several hours away. I'll wait."

"She's not going to be here at all today. Might not be here tomorrow either. You ought to go back to D.C."

Marge continued to stonewall Patrick, until he got fed up and drove away. He headed straight to the clinic and walked into Joey's examination room without knocking.

Joey was struggling with a very large and overly friendly Great Dane. "What the hell are you doing here?" he barked when he saw Patrick. "You should go home."

"Don't you start in on that too. I just got finished with Marge. I want to know where Robin is. I've got to talk to her one more time. I've got to make her understand."

"She's out of town. And you ought to go home."

"Why are you both nagging at me to go home?"

Joey stopped struggling long enough to say. "For once in your life, just trust me on this. Go home."

"Not till I see Robin."

"Trick! I said go home. I promise you'll understand everything. Please."

Patrick dug his car keys out of his pocket and stomped off to his car. He gunned the engine out of frustration before taking off.

Where was Robin? Was this all part of some elaborate ruse to enable her to avoid him? Was it that she couldn't even stand the sight of him? The questions bedeviled him all the way back to his place. He climbed the stairs to the second floor, his footsteps echoing heavy with fatigue, frustration and fear. What was it going to take to win her back? Could he do it?

When he got to the top of the stairs, he nearly tripped over a trim jean-clad leg. "Robin?"

"Oh, hullo. I was beginning to wonder if you were coming home."

Thank God she didn't look nearly as nonchalant as she sounded, he thought, then said, "Why are you here?" He wondered if she could hear the words over the deafening thud of his heart.

Robin scrambled to her feet and pulled a folded newspaper out of her back pocket. She waved it under Patrick's nose. "What's the meaning of this?"

His stomach clenched when he saw it was the article he'd written. Had he inadvertently caused even more trouble for her? "God, I'm sorry, honey."

"For what?"

"For—for whatever—whatever trouble the article—"

"You want to see exactly what that article has done?" She handed him a large envelope.

Totally confused, Patrick opened it. A few checks fell out of the overstuffed packet and drifted to the floor. He bent down to pick them up, whistling when he saw one check for a thousand dollars. "Wha—?"

"What your article did was bring in thousands of dollars in donations. Apparently, some people don't care what my husband did. They're just interested in what *I* do." She smiled timidly, then lowered her gaze to stare at the top of her boots.

"Then—" He cleared his tight throat. "You forgive me?"

"If you'll forgive me." When he heard her quiet words, relief flooded through him, leaving his knees weak and his eyes ablaze. Pulling her into his arms, he held her tight, as though to absorb her essence into his very being.

"It was a beautiful article," she murmured next to his ear. "Did you mean what you said?"

"Every word." He buried his face in her hair and reveled in its spring-sweet fragrance. His hands moved restlessly up and down her back, relearning the precious contours. It was several minutes before he finally pulled back long enough to see her face. Her smile glittered through her tears like sunshine sparkling through dewdrops.

He was overwhelmed at the need that rushed through him—the primitive need of a man to reclaim his territory, to show his woman that she belonged to him. And he to her.

He fumbled with his key, then opened his door and swept Robin up into his arms. "Be warned that I don't intend to let you back out until tomorrow morning. If then."

A joyous smile spread over Robin's face, and she looped her arms around his neck. "Maybe I won't let *you* out."

"I can only hope." He kicked the door shut behind him, then carried her straight to his bedroom. He set her down next to the bed, then began pulling at his clothes.

His jerky movements showed more desperation than finesse, but Robin didn't care. More than anything in the world, right now she needed him to wipe away the memories of all the nights without him.

"I've missed you so, honey, and I've needed you so, I don't think I can be slow this time," he groaned.

"Don't be slow." Robin ran her hands down his bare chest to his belt buckle.

When she slid his zipper down, Patrick sucked in his breath and laid his hands over hers. Funny, her hands were shaking. Or was it his hands? He looked down. Both pairs of hands.

Quickly, he shucked his jeans, then tugged hers off as well. When her fingers began unbuttoning her blouse, he stopped her, running his fingers over the pink satin. "Leave it on."

He lay with her on the bed and pulled her tightly into his arms. He just held her for the longest time, overwhelmed by love and relief. "God, honey, don't ever shut me out again. Please. Yell at me, hit me, kick me if you have to, but don't shut me out."

His hands smoothed over the pink satin, cupping her breasts and toying with the pouting nipples through the slick fabric. "Say you wore this for me."

"Yes, yes, I did." She whimpered beneath his demanding caress. "Please, Patrick, hurry."

"I changed my mind," Patrick murmured, moving his mouth on the cloth over her nipple. "I want it slow."

"Well, I didn't change mine!" With a deft movement she caught him off guard and pushed him onto his back. A wicked smile curved her lips as she took him into her body. "We'll do it slow later."

"All night," Patrick agreed with a gasp, and surged upward. "God, I love you, Robin McKenna."

"And I love you, Patrick Brady."

Temporarily spent, Patrick cuddled Robin against his chest, not willing to let even an inch separate any part of their bodies. "If I ever go through another three weeks like we just went through, I'll lose what's left of my mind."

Robin raised her head and looked down at him. "So will I. I don't plan on letting you out of my sight any longer than I have to."

Patrick's hands caressed her back, slipping up and down on the satin. "I'm sorry that I called Bill Marsh, Robin. I don't know how I can ever make it up to you."

"I can think of a way." Robin gently tugged at a curl on his chest. "When I get my wildlife center in operation, I'm going to need lots of help. I could always sentence you to a couple of years of community service." She looked up, her eyes pure gold with love and need.

His throat tightened with emotion. "If you're going to sentence me, honey, go all the way and make it for life. Please, make it for life."

EPILOGUE

The wedding was held in the meadow behind Robin's cabin and if three-legged raccoons stole crumbs off the buffet table and one-winged ducks followed the groom around, nobody thought anything of it. After all, this was the future site of the Needle Ridge Wildlife Care and Education Center.

And if, as soon as they were pronounced man and wife, the groom picked up the bride in his arms and dashed to his car just because she wore pink satin, nobody thought anything of that either. After all he was a city boy and they had some pretty strange notions.

THE EDITOR'S CORNER

Dear Readers,

If you loved our **BAD BOYS** last year, wait till you get a taste of our November LOVESWEPTs: **DANGEROUS MEN!** From a mysterious undercover state trooper to a roguish football player and a wilder-than-wild oil field wildcatter, these men thrive on danger, live on the edge, and push passion right past the limit! Like our heroines, you'll find it impossible to resist the sheer thrill of a walk on the wild side with men who are definitely *not* what your mother had in mind! With bold seduction and promises of passion, November's six heroes will sweep our heroines—and you—off your feet and into the fantasy of being loved by a Dangerous Man. . . .

Leanne Banks has created our first Dangerous Man in the sultry tale she calls **DANCE WITH THE DEVIL**, LOVESWEPT #648. Garth Pendleton was a bad boy who was definitely out of Erin Lindsey's league. Everything about him was a dare and Erin trembled at the danger of caring for a man whose darkest secret was tangled with her own shadowed past. Garth felt he'd waited for Erin forever and wanted to give her back her lost dreams, but if she knew the pain that haunted him, he feared the woman who'd slipped inside his lonely heart might slip away. This tempting tale is sure to please all of you who helped to make Leanne's January 1993 LOVESWEPT a #1 bestseller.

Doris Parmett's electrifying heroes and heroines have never been so highly-charged as they are in **BAD ATTITUDE**, LOVESWEPT #649. Reid Cameron was a heartbreaker cop who kissed like the hero of a hot romance. He'd invaded Polly Sweet's privacy—and her fantasies—when he'd commandeered her house to catch a jewel thief, but when he decided they'd play lovers and then tried to teach the feisty spitfire a lesson about feigning passion, both were shocked by the fireworks their lips set off! Doris is in top form with this sizzling story.

Longtime favorite author Patt Bucheister will tempt and tease you to distraction with her **TAME A WILDCAT**, LOVESWEPT #650. Ryder Knight had always thrived on the adventure of being a wildcatter, relished the pursuit of a new oil well, but he felt his restlessness vanish when Hannah Corbett told him he looked like trouble—and that he was no gentleman! But when his possessive embrace made her go up in flames, she feared losing control, trading her freedom for the joy only he could teach her. Patt will keep you on the edge of your seat for every page of this one!

We at LOVESWEPT are always pleased to welcome a talented new writer to our pages, and we're sure you'll agree that Donna Kauffman, author of

ILLEGAL MOTION, LOVESWEPT #651, is as good as they come. Football star Nick Logan was desperate enough to try anything to clear his name, and he figured he could intimidate or charm the truth out of Willa Trask—until he was burned by the sparks that flared between him and the beautiful redhead! He'd hired her to rehabilitate his injured knee, vowing to discover if she'd helped frame him—but instead of an ice princess, he found in her a wanton witch who touched his soul. When you've read this winning story, I'm sure you'll become big fans of Donna Kauffman!

We turn from a rookie to an all-star pro for our next Dangerous Man. Let the heartbreaking emotion of Laura Taylor sweep you away with **WILDER'S WOMAN**, LOVESWEPT #652. Craig Wilder—uncivilized, untamed, he'd paid a high price for survival. He'd meant to teach Chelsea Lockridge a lesson, to punish his ex-wife for her betrayal, but he hadn't anticipated the erotic torment of molding his body to hers—nor imagined the tenderness still buried deep inside his battered heart! She'd braved the wilderness and a storm with evidence that could deliver the justice Craig had been denied, but Chelsea wanted to prove she'd never lost faith in him . . . or her reckless passion for the man who could make her purr with pleasure. Branded for all eternity by a lover whose scars ran deep, she vowed she could help Craig mourn the past and trust her again by fighting his demons with the sweet fury of her love. Laura's deeply moving tale will capture you, heart and soul.

If you like your men *truly* dangerous, Glenna McReynolds has the mystery man for you in **AVENGING ANGEL**, LOVESWEPT #653. Bruised and bloody, Dylan Jones has driven a thousand miles with her name on his lips, desperate to save Johanna Lane from being murdered! The secrets she knew made her a target, and he was her best chance of getting out alive—even if it meant abducting the lady and keeping her with him against her will. Frightened and furious, Johanna was stunned to realize she knew her captor . . . and once had even desired him! Dylan gambled his life to feel her heat and taste the forbidden fruit of her lips and Johanna longed to repay the debt. I can't think of a better way to end your month of **DANGEROUS MEN** than with Glenna's **AVENGING ANGEL!**

So hang on to your hearts—next month six **DANGEROUS MEN** are coming to steal them away!

Happy reading,

Nita Taublib

Nita Taublib

Associate Publisher

P.S. Don't miss the exciting women's fiction Bantam has coming in November—sensual seduction in Susan Johnson's **OUTLAW**; love and black magic over the centuries in **MOONLIGHT, MADNESS, AND MAGIC** by LOVESWEPT authors Suzanne Forster, Charlotte Hughes, and Olivia Rupprecht; and a classic Fayrene Preston romance, **SATIN AND STEELE**. We'll be giving you a sneak peek at these terrific books in next month's LOVESWEPTs. And immediately following this page, look for a preview of the spectacular women's fiction books from Bantam *available now!*

Teresa Medeiros

nationally bestselling author of
ONCE AN ANGEL
and HEATHER AND VELVET

presents

A WHISPER OF ROSES

"From humor to adventure, poignancy to passion, tenderness to sensuality, Teresa Medeiros writes rare love stories to cherish."—*Romantic Times*

Set in the wild Highlands of Scotland, this captivating historical romance is bursting with the breathtaking passion, sparkling humor, and enchanting atmosphere that have made Teresa Medeiros a bestselling author. It tells the heartbreaking tale of two lovers torn between their passion and the clan rivalry that divides their families.

The door behind him crashed open into the opposite wall, and Morgan swung around to find himself facing yet another exotic creature of myth.

A princess, her cloud of dark hair tumbled loose around her shoulders, the light behind her throwing every curve beneath her ivory nightdress into magnificent relief. Her delicate fingers were curled not around a scepter, but around the engraved hilt of a ceremonial claymore.

Silvery fingers of moonlight caressed the five feet of steel that lay between her hands and his heart.

"Hold your ground, rogue MacDonnell," she sweetly snarled. "One careless step and I'll be forced to take your head downstairs without the rest of you."

Morgan didn't even feel the pain as the crystal rose

snapped in his clumsy hands, embedding its stem deep in his palm.

"Why, you clumsy oaf! Look what you've gone and done now!"

Morgan's gaze automatically dropped to his hands. A jagged shard of glass protruded from his palm. Warm blood trickled down his wrist and forearm to puddle on one of Elizabeth Cameron's precious rugs. Before he could quench it, the old shame flared. Shame for being a MacDonnell. Shame for being such a crude ox. Just as quickly on its heels followed rage—the crushing rage that shielded his tattered pride from every blow. But before he could unleash it on the hapless girl, she dropped the sword and rushed over to him.

Tossing the splintered remains of the rose aside without a second glance, she cradled his hand in hers and dabbed at the wound with a wad of her nightdress. Her little hand was warm and soft and silky smooth beneath his own. "You really should take more care," she chided. "If you'd have struck your wrist, you might have bled to death."

Morgan was too dumbfounded by her concern to point out her illogic. If she'd have cut off his head, he might have bled to death even quicker. Still scowling over his hand, she dragged him toward the pale circle of light at the window.

"Be very still," she commanded. "I'm going to try to fish out this piece of glass. It's bound to be painful. You may scream if you like. I shan't think any less of you."

Since she'd never thought much of him to begin with, Morgan wasn't concerned. He didn't even flinch when she pressed his palm with her thumb and snagged the sliver of glass between the polished crescents of her fingernails.

Thoroughly bemused, Morgan studied her in the moonlight. The top of her head barely came to his chest. The spiral curls he used to yank with such relish tumbled down her back in inky waves. Her skin was fair except for the faintest hint of color, as if God had brushed rose petals across her cheeks and lips. A fringe of ebony silk shuttered her eyes. Her scent filled his nostrils, and he was shocked to feel his throat tighten with a primal hunger. She smelled like her mother, but fresher, sweeter. Some primitive male instinct warned him this was a bloom still on the vine, fragrant and tender and ripe. He frowned. She might be nectar to another man, but to him, Dougal Cameron's daughter would be as deadly as nightshade.

Her teeth cut into her lower lip as if to bite back a cry of her own as she drew forth the shard of glass and stanched the bleeding with yet another wad of her nightdress. Morgan feared he might soon have more of it twined around his arm than she had around her body. But an intriguing glimpse of a slender calf silenced his protest.

Grimacing, she lay the bloody splinter on the window-sill before glancing up at him.

At that moment, he cocked his head to the side, giving her an unobstructed view of his face. Moonlight melted over its harsh planes and angles, etching its alien virility in ruthless lines. He was a stranger, yet so hauntingly familiar she couldn't stop her hand from lifting, her fingertips from brushing the stubborn jut of his jaw. His eyes were guarded, like the forest at dusk.

"Hello, brat," he said.

Then she felt that old, familiar kick in the stomach and knew she was standing face to face in the moonlit tower with Morgan MacDonnell, his boyish promise of masculine beauty come to devastating fruition.

Mortified by her own boldness, she snatched her hand back, remembering another time she had touched him in tenderness and he had rubuked her in anger.

A wry grin touched his lips. "I suppose if you'd have known it was me, you'd have let me bleed to death."

Terrified she was going to revert to a stammering six-year-old, she snapped, "Of course not. You were dripping all over Mama's Flemish rug."

To hide her consternation, she lowered her gaze back to his hand. That was a mistake for she could not help staring, fascinated by the blunt size of his fingers, the warmth of his work-roughened skin, the rhythmic throb of his pulse beneath her thumb. She had the absurd thought that it must take a mighty heart indeed to fuel such a man.

"You've grown," she blurted out accusingly.

"So have you."

His low, amused tone warned her. She looked up to find his gaze taking a leisurely jaunt up her body, finally coming to rest with bold regard on her face. A splinter of anger twisted in her heart. For so long she had yearned for him to look at her with affection. But why now, when she sensed his admiration might be even more lethal to her than enmity?

Hardly aware of her actions, she tore a strip of priceless Chinese silk from her mother's drapes and wrapped it around his palm. "So what were you doing up here? Plotting a massacre? Trying to find a way to lower the harpsichord out the window? Searching for a mouse to put in my bed?"

Lucky mouse, Morgan thought, but he wisely refrained from saying so. "If you must know, lass, I was searchin' for a moment's peace."

"Ha!" She knotted the bandage with a crisp jerk that finally drew a flinch from him. "Peace and the MacDonnells hardly go hand in hand."

"Fine talk from a lass who just burst in here threatenin' to cut off my head."

Sabrina could hardly argue with the truth of that.

He jerked his head toward the door. "Why aren't you down there with the rest of your family, lordin' your noble gestures over the poor peasants?"

Morgan's size might have changed, but not the rest of him. Resenting his uncanny knack of making her feel ashamed of who she was, she gave a dainty snort. "Peasants, indeed. Barefoot savages, the lot of them. Mama would have been better off serving them at a trough instead of a table."

His voice was quiet, its very lack of emotion a rebuke of its own. "If their table manners aren't to your likin', it might be because most of them won't see that much food again in their lifetimes. And their feet are bare because they're savin' the rotted soles of their boots for the cold winter months. They don't lose as many toes that way."

Shame buffeted her. Sabrina dropped her gaze, then wished she hadn't as it fell on the stark lines of Morgan's bare legs and feet. Golden hair dusted his muscular calves. His soles must be as tough as leather to bear the stony soil of the mountainside without protection. Her own toes curled sheepishly into the plush cashmere of her stockings.

"I begged Mama to let me join the festivities," she confessed.

"Why didn't you appeal to your dotin' papa? As I recall,

he never could resist a flutter of those pretty little lashes of yours."

Sabrina's gaze shot to his face. Morgan had never given her any indication that he'd noticed her lashes before. "Even Papa was adamant this time." A soft chuckle escaped her. "It seems your reputations preceded you. He was terrified one of you might hit me over the head and drag me off by my hair."

Morgan was silent for so long that she feared she'd offended him again. Then he reached down and lifted a skein of her hair in his uninjured hand, rubbing it between thumb and forefinger. A dreamy languor stole across her features. The cadence of Sabrina's heartbeat shifted in warning.

He let the stolen tendril ripple through his fingers in a cascade of midnight silk before turning the dusky heat of his gaze on her. "I can't say I blame him, lass. If you were mine, I'd probably lock you away, too."

If you were mine . . .

The words hung suspended between them, far more awkward than their silence. In a breath of utter lunacy, Sabrina wondered how it would feel to belong to a man like him, dared to ponder what came after being dragged off by her hair.

Caught in the same spell of moonlight and solitude, Morgan's gaze dropped to her parted lips. His starving senses reeled, intoxicated by the scent of roses that flared his nostrils, the cling of her hair against his callused knuckles. He'd long ago resigned himself to the harsh life of a Highland warrior. But this girl's softness awakened old hungers and weakened his resolve. He hadn't touched a drop of wine, yet he felt drunk, reckless. What harm could one kiss to? Resisting the temptation to plunge his tongue between her unwitting lips, he leaned down and touched his mouth to hers.

At the press of Morgan's lips against her own, Sabrina's eyes fluttered shut. His kiss was brief, dry, almost tentative, yet a melting sweetness unfolded within her. She felt the leashed power in his touch. Such gentleness in a man his size wove a spell all its own. Only in the last brief second of contact did he allow himself the wicked luxury of dragging his lips across hers, molding her beneath him in perfect harmony.

TENDER BETRAYAL
by
ROSANNE BITTNER

Bestselling author of OUTLAW HEARTS
and THUNDER ON THE PLAINS

"Bittner's characters are so finely drawn, their lives so
richly detailed, one cannot help but to care deeply for
each of them." —*Affaire de Coeur*

*When Audra Brennan savored her first, forbidden taste of
desire in the arms of handsome lawyer Lee Jeffreys, his
caresses sparked a flame within that burned away the differ-
ences between rebel and Yankee.*

The shelling from the bigger guns seemed to have
stopped. She decided that at least until daylight she had no
choice but to stay here as Lee had directed. She went back
to the cot and lay down, breathing his scent on his pillow
and sheets. How odd that she felt so safe in this bed where
a Yankee soldier slept. She was in the center of the enemy
camp, yet she was not afraid.

She drifted off to sleep, losing all track of time. Finally
someone knocked gently on the rear door. "Audra? It's
me."

Audra rubbed at her eyes, holding the shirt around
herself as she found her way to the door. It was still dark.
"Lee?"

"Let me in. The worst is over."

Audra obeyed, and Lee turned and latched the door
again. Audra looked up at him, seeing blood on his right
arm. "You're hurt!"

"Nothing drastic. I told my commander I'd tend to it

myself. He doesn't know you're in here, and I don't want him to know just yet." He threw a bundle of clothes on the small table on which the lamp was sitting. "I looted those out of a clothing store like a common thief. I don't know your size. I just took a guess. You've got to have something to wear when you leave here."

Lee removed his jacket and boots, then began unbuttoning his shirt. "It's a madhouse out there. Most of the men have chased the rebels back into the countryside, and they're looting through town like crazy men. It's practically impossible to keep any of these men in line. They aren't regular army, just civilian volunteers, for the most part, come here to teach the rebels a lesson. They don't know a damn thing about real military conduct or how to obey orders." He glanced at her. "I still intend to have the bastards who attacked you whipped. How do you feel?"

She sat down on the cot, suddenly self-conscious now that she was more rested. She had removed her shoes and stockings and wore only his shirt and her bloomers. "Just terribly tired and . . . I don't know . . . numb, I guess. It's all so ugly and unreal."

"That's war, Audra, ugly and unreal. You asked me once what it's like. Now you know." He peeled off his bloodstained shirt, and Audra found herself studying his muscular arms and the familiar broad chest, the dark hair that lightly dusted that chest and led downward in a V shape past the belt of his pants. He walked to the stand that still held a bowl of water and he poured some fresh water into it, then wet a rag and held it to the cut on his arm, which was already scabbing over. "Some rebel tried to stab me with his bayonet. Missed what he was aiming for by a long shot, but he didn't miss me all together, obviously."

"Let me help you."

"Don't worry about it. It isn't bleeding anymore." He washed his face and neck, then dried off and picked up a flask of whiskey. He opened it and poured some over the cut, grimacing at the sting of it. Then he swallowed some of the whiskey straight from the flask. "They say whiskey is supposed to help ease pain," he said then. "It does, but only physical pain. It doesn't do a thing for the pain in a man's heart."

She looked away. "Lee, don't—"

"Why not? In a couple of days you'll go back to Brennan Manor, and I'll go on with what I have to do, because I'm bound to do it and it isn't in me to be a deserter, no matter the reason. You have to stay near home because it's the only way you're going to know what happened to Joey, and you'll want to be there when he comes home, God willing. Who knows what will happen when all this is over? In the meantime I've found you again, and I need to tell you I love you, Audra. I never stopped loving you and I probably never will."

Audra held back tears. Why was he saying this now, when it was impossible for them to be together? Everything had changed. They were not the same people as they'd been that summer at Maple Shadows, and besides that, it was wrong to be sitting here half-undressed in front of the man she'd slept with while married to someone else, wasn't it? It was wrong to care this much about a Yankee. *All* of this was wrong, but then, what was right anymore?

He set the flask down on the table. "This might really be it, Audra; the end for you and me. But we have tonight."

"Why is it always that way for us? It was like that at Maple Shadows, and that one night you came to visit. All we ever have is one night, Lee, never knowing what will come tomorrow. I can't do that again. It hurts too much, and it's wrong."

Audra looked away as Lee began to undress. "Please take me somewhere, Lee, anywhere away from here."

He came over to kneel in front of her, grasping her wrists. "There *is* no place to take you, not tonight. And it's *not* wrong, Audra. It was *never* wrong, and you know it. And this time it isn't just tonight. When this is over, I'm coming back, and we're going to be together, do you hear me? I'm not going to live like this the rest of my life. I want you, Audra, and dammit, you want *me*! We've both known it since that first day you came here to see me, widow or not! Maybe this *is* the last chance we'll have to be together, but as God is my witness, if I don't get killed or so badly wounded that I can't come to you, I'll be back to find you, and we're going to put this war behind us!"

She looked at him pleadingly. "That's impossible now," she said in a near whisper.

"That isn't true. You just don't want to *believe* that it's possible, because it makes you feel like a traitor." He leaned closer. "Well, then, *I'm* a traitor, too! Because while my men are out there chasing and killing rebels, I'll be in here making *love* to one!"

Why couldn't she object, argue, remember why she should say no? Why was she never able to resist this man she should have hated?

"I never said anything about making love," she whispered.

He searched her green eyes, eyes that had told him all along how much she wanted him again. "You didn't have to," he answered.

THE PAINTED LADY
by
LUCIA GRAHAME

This is a stunningly sensual first novel about sexual awakening set in nineteenth-century France and England. Romantic Times *called it "a unique and rare reading experience."*

This wonderfully entertaining novel showcases the superb writing talents of Lucia Grahame. With lyric simplicity and beauty THE PAINTED LADY will entrance you from first page to last. Read on to discover an exquisite story about a proud, dark-haired woman and her hidden desire that is finally freed.

"If I stay longer with you tonight," Anthony said, his words seeming to reach me through a thick mist, "it will be on one condition. You will not balk at *anything* I ask of you. I leave it to you. I will go now and count tonight to your account, since, although you were occasionally dilatory, you acquitted yourself well enough, for the most part. Or I will stay, on *my* conditions—but at *your* wish. It rests with you. Do I stay or go?"

"Stay," I whispered.

I swayed and jingled as he led me back to the hearthside and laid me down upon the pillows.

"Undress me," he commanded when we were stretched out before the fire. "Slowly. As slowly as you can."

I moved closer to him and began to unfasten the buttons of his waistcoat.

He sighed.

"Don't rush," he whispered. "I can feel how eager you are, but try to control yourself. Take your time."

It was maddening to force myself to that unhurried

pace, but in the end it only sharpened my hunger. As I contemplated the climactic pleasures in store—who could have said how long it would take to achieve them?—I could not help savoring the small but no less sweet ones immediately at hand. The slight drag against my skin of the fine wool that clothed him, more teasing even than I had imagined it; the almost imperceptible fragrance of lavender that wafted from his shirt, the hands which lay so lightly upon my waist as I absorbed the knowledge that the task he had set for me was not an obstacle to fulfillment but a means of enhancing it.

Yet I had unbuttoned only his waistcoat and his shirt when he told me to stop. He drew back from me a little. The very aura of controlled desire he radiated made me long to submerge myself in the impersonal heat and forgetfulness that his still presence next to me both promised and withheld.

I moved perhaps a centimeter closer to him.

"No," he said.

He began, in his calm, unhasty way, to remove his remaining clothing himself. I steadied my breath a little and watched the firelight move like a sculptor's fingers over his cool, hard body.

At last he leaned over me, but without touching me.

"You're so compliant tonight," he said almost tenderly. "You must be very hungry for your freedom, *mon fleur du miel*."

I felt a twist of sadness. For an instant, I thought he had used Frederick's nickname for me. But he had called me something quite different—a flower, not of evil, but of sweetness . . . honey.

He brought his hand to my cheek and stroked it softly. I closed my eyes. Only the sudden sharp intake of my breath could have told him of the effect of that light touch.

He bent his head. I caught the scents of mint and smoke and my own secrets as his mouth moved close to mine.

I tipped my head back and opened my lips.

How long I had resisted those kisses! Now I craved his mouth, wanting to savor and prolong every sensation that could melt away my frozen, imprisoning armor of misery and isolation.

He barely grazed my lips with his.

Then he pulled himself to his knees and gently coaxed me into the same position, facing him.

Keeping his lips lightly on mine, he reached out and took my shoulders gently to bring me closer. My breasts brushed his chest with every long, shivering breath I took.

"You are free now," whispered my husband at last, releasing me, "to do as you like. . . . How will you use your liberty?"

For an answer, I put my arms around his neck, sank back upon the pillows, pulling him down to me, and brought my wild mouth to his. . . .

OREGON BROWN
by
SARA ORWIG

Bestselling author of TIDES OF PASSION
and NEW ORLEANS

"The multi-faceted talent of Sara Orwig gleams as
bright as gold." —*Rave Reviews*

*With more than five million copies of her books in print,
Sara Orwig is without a doubt one of romance's top authors.
Her previous novels have been showered with praise and
awards, including five* Romantic Times *awards and nu-
merous* Affaire de Coeur *awards.*

*Now Bantam Books is proud to present a new edition of one
of her most passionate novels—the story of a woman forced to
choose between fantasy and reality. . . .*

Charity Webster left the city for small-town Oklahoma
to assume the reins of the family company she had
inherited. With nothing behind her but a failed business and a shattered romance, and no one in her new
life except an aging aunt, Charity gives her nights to a
velvet-voiced late-night deejay . . . and to a fantasy
about the man behind the sexy, sultry voice.

But daylight brings her into head-on conflict with
another man, the wealthy O. O. Brown, who is maneuvering to acquire the family firm. Arrogant and all too
aware of his own charm, he still touches off a sensuous
spark in Charity that she can't deny . . . and she finds
herself torn between two men—one a mystery, the
other the keeper of her deepest secrets.

OFFICIAL RULES

To enter the sweepstakes below carefully follow all instructions found elsewhere in this offer.

The **Winners Classic** will award prizes with the following approximate maximum values: 1 Grand Prize: $26,500 (or $25,000 cash alternate); 1 First Prize: $3,000; 5 Second Prizes: $400 each; 35 Third Prizes: $100 each; 1,000 Fourth Prizes: $7.50 each. Total maximum retail value of Winners Classic Sweepstakes is $42,500. Some presentations of this sweepstakes may contain individual entry numbers corresponding to one or more of the aforementioned prize levels. To determine the Winners, individual entry numbers will first be compared with the winning numbers preselected by computer. For winning numbers not returned, prizes will be awarded in random drawings from among all eligible entries received. Prize choices may be offered at various levels. If a winner chooses an automobile prize, all license and registration fees, taxes, destination charges and, other expenses not offered herein are the responsibility of the winner. If a winner chooses a trip, travel must be complete within one year from the time the prize is awarded. Minors must be accompanied by an adult. Travel companion(s) must also sign release of liability. Trips are subject to space and departure availability. Certain black-out dates may apply.

The following applies to the sweepstakes named above:

No purchase necessary. You can also enter the sweepstakes by sending your name and address to: P.O. Box 508, Gibbstown, N.J. 08027. Mail each entry separately. Sweepstakes begins 6/1/93. Entries must be received by 12/30/94. Not responsible for lost, late, damaged, misdirected, illegible or postage due mail. Mechanically reproduced entries are not eligible. All entries become property of the sponsor and will not be returned.

Prize Selection/Validations: Selection of winners will be conducted no later than 5:00 PM on January 28, 1995, by an independent judging organization whose decisions are final. Random drawings will be held at 1211 Avenue of the Americas, New York, N.Y. 10036. Entrants need not be present to win. Odds of winning are determined by total number of entries received. Circulation of this sweepstakes is estimated not to exceed 200 million. All prizes are guaranteed to be awarded and delivered to winners. Winners will be notified by mail and may be required to complete an affidavit of eligibility and release of liability which must be returned within 14 days of date on notification or alternate winners will be selected in a random drawing. Any prize notification letter or any prize returned to a participating sponsor, Bantam Doubleday Dell Publishing Group, Inc., its participating divisions or subsidiaries, or the independent judging organization as undeliverable will be awarded to an alternate winner. Prizes are not transferable. No substitution for prizes except as offered or as may be necessary due to unavailability, in which case a prize of equal or greater value will be awarded. Prizes will be awarded approximately 90 days after the drawing. All taxes are the sole responsibility of the winners. Entry constitutes permission (except where prohibited by law) to use winners' names, hometowns, and likenesses for publicity purposes without further or other compensation. Prizes won by minors will be awarded in the name of parent or legal guardian.

Participation: Sweepstakes open to residents of the United States and Canada, except for the province of Quebec. Sweepstakes sponsored by Bantam Doubleday Dell Publishing Group, Inc., (BDD), 1540 Broadway, New York, NY 10036. Versions of this sweepstakes with different graphics and prize choices will be offered in conjunction with various solicitations or promotions by different subsidiaries and divisions of BDD. Where applicable, winners will have their choice of any prize offered at level won. Employees of BDD, its divisions, subsidiaries, advertising agencies, independent judging organization, and minors, and their immediate family members are not eligible.

Canadian residents, in order to win, must first correctly answer a time limited arithmetical skill testing question. Void in Puerto Rico, Quebec and wherever prohibited or restricted by law. Subject to all federal, state, local and provincial laws and regulations. For a list of major prize winners (available after 1/29/95): send a self-addressed, stamped envelope entirely separate from your entry to: Sweepstakes Winners, P.O. Box 517, Gibbstown, NJ 08027. Requests must be received by 12/30/94. DO NOT SEND ANY OTHER CORRESPONDENCE TO THIS P.O. BOX.